THE CONNOISSEURS

A PLAY

By ED STRUM

REMDUST PUBLISHING
The Connoisseurs, Copyright © 2024 by Ed Strum
All Rights Reserved
ISBN 978-0-9913897-0-4

2010 Winner Robert J. Pickering Award for Playwriting Excellence

Final Four - 2010 Lionheart Theatre's "Make The House Roar" Contest

Finalist – 2011 Mountain Playhouse Int'l Comedy Playwriting Contest

Books by Ed Strum

THE CONNOISSSEURS – A Play

MONTOBA – A Novel

THE BURROW & THE GREAT PANDEMIC, A Play

JOURNEY OF THE SCROLLS – A Novel

JOURNEY OF THE SCROLLS – SPECIAL EDITION

THE PRINCESS OF ÉLEVÉ – A Play

EVERY DAY IS A GOOD DAY – A Play

THE HOLLOW PENCIL – A Play

CASCADIA and THE GREAT PANDEMIC – A Novel

ADAM'S ARK & THE GREAT PANDEMIC – A Play

RICHIE   A Poetic Play in One Scene

A SENSORY FEAST – An Anthology of Prose Poetry

THE

CONNOISSEURS

ACTOR'S EDITION

A COMEDY

Acknowledgements

Many thanks to Leslie Brown, Heather Strum and Jim Jacobs for reviewing the play numerous times and suggesting various editing changes. Thanks also to Philip Burton of Burton Jewelers, Anacortes, Washington, for a key suggestion early in the development process that spurred on subsequent research and his subsequent comments; to Beth Hudson who jumped in with her own suggestions and enthusiasm, and her research on various sources; to Heidi Lewis of the San Juan Island Library for finding many references and to Fred Silverstein for his comments.

My appreciation to the reading group of Gray Cope, Pam Gillette, Marcy Hahn, Barry Jacobson, Shannon Kelley, Ernest Pugh and Susan Ross. Hearing a play read by writers, actors, directors and playgoers provides insight into language, cadence and character. Your continuous laughter during the cold reading was rewarding and immensely helpful. Thanks also to Tammy Anderson, Kamela Chambers, Marcy Hahn and Charles Richardson who participated in the staged reading prior to the second production.

My thanks to Merritt Olsen and the San Juan Community Theatre for providing opportunities to writers for the development and production of monologues and one act plays, and for providing opportunities to directors and actors for their development. Each of these opportunities contributes to overall development of one's skills, whether as writer, director, actor or producer of theatre.

My great appreciation to the cast, crew, director and producer at the Branch County Community Theatre for their performance of the World Premiere of this play.

My very special thanks to Merritt Olsen for his analysis, insight, extensive comments and suggestions prior to and during the production process of the West Coast Premiere.

Finally, my great appreciation to the cast, crew and director at the SJ Community Theatre for their production of the West Coast Premiere of this play.

Production History

The World Premiere Production of "The Connoisseurs" was March, 2010 by the Branch County Community Theatre (Producer: Jennifer Colbeck) at the Tibbits Opera House in Coldwater, Michigan. The production was directed by J. Richard Colbeck; the set was by J R and Jennifer Colbeck, Marc Pebernat, Hans and Jackie Jonsson, Larry Downs, and Ann and Jadon Brois, the costume design and properties by Ann Brois and Deborah Jersey, the lighting design by David Brown, the sound design by Ken Delaney, and the stage manager and assistant stage manager were Larry and Judy Downs. The cast was:

George Sable	Aaron Paul
Lynn Sable	Teresa Maurer
Al Hunter	Matt Sargent
Peggy Hunter	Jackie Jonsson
Mrs. Herald	Irene Grimes-Butdorf
Wine Owner	Dave Winn
US Coast Guard Woman	Carla Ram
Mr. Big	Larry Stewart
Voices	Ann Brois, Deb Jersey

The West Coast Premiere of "The Connoisseurs" was July 23, 2010 at the San Juan County Community Theatre in Friday Harbor, Washington. The production was directed by Merritt Olsen; the stage manager and sound board operator was Vanessa Johnson; the assistant stage manager was Gene Bornholdt; the set and designer was Steve Judson; the light designer and light board operator was John Shaller; the scenic artists were Jane Maxwell Campbell and Lyne McPherson; the set painters were Kyle Aberle, Jane Huestis and Gayle Hyland; the set construction and light crew were John Aberle, Dennis Busse, Henry Busse, Tom Donnelly, Greg Findley, Craig Green, Mike Killion, Conrad Shaller, John Shaller and Robert Sharp; the stage crew were Sheila Harley and Pete Dawson; the property master was Ted Soares; the costume designer was Marilyn Findley; the pantomime coordinator was Julie Laidlaw; the fight master was Lisa Moretti. Holly Harbers, Denny Holm and Ellen Roberts recorded rehearsals. The cast was:

George Sable	George Iliff
Lynn Sable	Margaret Hall
Al Hunter	Bo Turnage
Peggy Hunter	Lisa Moretti
Mrs. Herald	Pat Rishel
Wine Owner	Warren Baehr
US Coast Guard Lady	Meredith Block
Mr. Big	Roberto Carrieri
Sheriff and Voices	Gene Bornholdt

THE CONNOISSEURS

CAST OF CHARACTERS
(In order of appearance)

George Sable – old enough to know a bit about wine
Loves and lives for wine

Lynn, his wife
Loves and knows jewelry; unflappable, takes charge

Al Hunter
Loveable, loyal, "life of the party", doomsayer but comes through when necessary

Peggy, his wife
Loves danger, risk-taker, vivacious, intuitive

Mrs. Herald, a neighbor – (any age/gender) - Busybody with secret

Wine Owner – any age (or gender)

US Coast Guard Lady – any age (female)

Mr. Big – any age (or gender)

Sheriff – any age/gender, (double cast with Mrs. H, CGL, WO or Mr. Big)
Note: Sheriff can be off-stage for two brief appearances, need not be cast
Cast - 7 if double casting of Coast Guard Lady with WO or Mr. Big
        6 (double casting of WO with CGL and Mrs. H with Mr. Big)
The action takes place in the main room of the home of George and Lynn, situated on a strait connected to the ocean. It's a warm day in April, 2004.

Running Time: 90 – 100 Minutes

THE CONNOISSEURS

ACT ONE

The room has a deck outside which leads down to the beach. Opposite the deck is the front door entrance. An exit leads to bedrooms and bathrooms, and another exit leads to the kitchen, the laundry room and the garage. It is important that only the exit to the kitchen is seen. The laundry room and garage are implied in the script.

As an example, the deck/beach can be at the fourth wall (i.e., the audience), with access including wings and curtain ends. The front door is center upstage, the kitchen SR and the bedrooms SL. The set includes a telescope pointed at the water, an easy chair, a VHF, a phone, a computer, a sofa, coffee table, small table, tea service, magazine rack, a 2004 Pocket Wine Guide, Lynn's cell phone and a cabinet or cupboard to hide wine. A bowl of agates sits on the coffee table. Collecting agates from beaches is Lynn's hobby.

Scene 1

George sits in the chair reading a wine magazine. He dresses casually. Lynn enters from the kitchen. She dresses elegantly, wearing a necklace, earrings, bracelet and ring. A bottle of Chablis Grande Cru sits on the cupboard. Dusk is settling in.

LYNN
The salmon's ready. I took it out. You have the wine?

GEORGE
I pulled a Chablis Grand Cru. '90 Vaudesir. On the cupboard.

LYNN
(*Looks toward water.*) George, have you noticed that boat out there?

He doesn't respond and continues looking through a wine magazine.

GEORGE
Ummm!

1

LYNN

It came through the pass 20 minutes ago. It's behaving strangely.

GEORGE

(Intent on magazine) Boy, I'd like a few of those in my wine cellar!

LYNN

It was running against the current then it stopped. It's just sitting there, drifting slowly.

GEORGE

You should see this. Remember that '45 port we had years ago? It was...

LYNN

(Interrupts sharply.) You haven't heard a word I've said!

GEORGE

Hmmm!

LYNN

It's getting dark. His running lights are on but he isn't moving.

GEORGE

This '78 Châteauneuf-du-Pape is terrific. Reminds me of my first ones, '55s and '59s.

LYNN

The lights are dimmer and lower in the water.

GEORGE

Oh?

He perks up a bit, returns to magazine. She looks through the scope.

LYNN

The boat's sinking! Take a look.

GEORGE

What?

He jumps up and rushes over to her, suddenly energized.

LYNN
I see two people swimming to the other side of the pass.

GEORGE
Why that island instead of this one?

LYNN
It's a shorter swim, George. No current to cross?

GEORGE
(Grabs scope.) My Lord! They must've hit something – or swamped.

LYNN
Maybe they hit a log?

GEORGE
The current's strong through the pass now, three or four knots, I'd say.

LYNN
You see the people?

GEORGE
Yeah! They're at the shore. *(Thinks, looks at VHF.)* That's strange.

LYNN
What's strange?

GEORGE
There was nothing on the VHF. Why didn't they call May Day?

LYNN
Maybe they didn't have time?

Al runs in from beach with a bottle of red wine in each hand.

AL
Hey, George! Look what came ashore.

GEORGE

Where'd you get those?

AL

Saw them bobbing off the point, drifting into the cove. Pulled them in.

GEORGE

They were floating?

AL

Not the bottles! They were inside a cardboard box sealed in plastic.

LYNN

How'd you know that?

AL

I opened one. Each case has 12 bottles packed in foam.

GEORGE

Ingenious! Made to float. *(Realizes what Al said.)* You say each case?

AL

There're dozens tied together with rope, just floating out there.

GEORGE

You know what you have there?

AL

Wine?

GEORGE

No! I mean - these are priceless. '86 Mouton Rothschild. '86 Latour.

AL

There're lots more off the beach.

Lynn takes wine. George and Al run off. She puts bottles on cupboard, takes Chablis to kitchen, exits. Peggy runs in through front door.

PEGGY

Lynn? *(Lynn returns.)* Did you see those boxes bobbing out there?

LYNN

Al saw them.

PEGGY

Looks like they're tied together. Where'd they come from?

LYNN

That boat. Look! It's sinking. Oh, it's gone now!

PEGGY

I wonder what's in those boxes?

LYNN

Just some old wine. Al brought in two bottles to show to George.

PEGGY

Old wine?

LYNN

George says they're valuable. Then they ran out.

Peggy looks at Lynn, starts to run to the beach, meets Al running in.

PEGGY

Al, what're you doing?

AL

Come and help! George's going crazy dragging all those boxes in.

PEGGY

All the boxes? How many?

AL

Hundreds! *(To Lynn)* You have an old tarp? Tan, natural looking?

LYNN

I suppose so. Why?

5

AL

We're stacking the boxes behind a big rock and covering them with a tarp and driftwood.

LYNN

Should be a rolled-up tarp just inside the garage.

AL

(Al runs to the kitchen door.) Help us Peggy. George is like a maniac. I'm afraid he'll have a heart attack. *(Exits.)*

PEGGY

Let's go Lynn!

LYNN

You go. I don't care about old wine, but if a box is filled with jewels...

Lynn flashes her diamond ring and bracelet, fingers her necklace and diamond earrings.

PEGGY

Jewels?

LYNN

I've loved them ever since I was a jeweler. I'm especially fond of diamonds.

PEGGY

Diamonds? Come on, Lynn! *(Playfully, she tries to drag Lynn out.)*

LYNN

How about a 1 or 2 carat, D color, flawless diamond?

PEGGY

Come on. Be serious.

LYNN

Round brilliant ideal cut. *(Lynn flashes her ring.)*

PEGGY

Lynn! This is thrilling! No telling what we'll find!

LYNN

A pirate's chest with stolen treasure? That'd excite me. Even agates. *(She picks one up.)*

PEGGY

Now you're talking. This'll be really exciting! *(She pulls Lynn gently.)*

Al runs back in. He has an old rolled up tarp under his arm.

AL

This the one?

LYNN

That's it. Do you need help?

AL

No, I can handle it.

Al runs out to the beach but the tarp unrolls behind him so he drags it through the room and down to the beach. He's unaware of this.

PEGGY

Wait Al! I'll help you. *(She chases after then returns.)* He's gone. Poor Al. *(She tries to pull Lynn out.)* Come on Lynn! They need our help.

LYNN

Oh, OK! *(They start but Lynn resists.)* But the salmon! It'll get cold.

PEGGY

The salmon can wait! *(She pulls her out as they exit to the beach.)*

Pantomime (optional - cross on or below apron of stage SR to SL) Lights dim, backlighting only. Four silhouetted figures tiptoe across edge of beach. Each carries a box of wine taking it from the beach to the stash behind the rock under the tarp.

Fast scene change. Light changes showing passage of time. It's later in the night. George and Al stumble in from the garage. Peggy shuffles in. All are disheveled and dirty from being out on the beach. Lynn drags herself in. Each holds a few bottles of wine, 10 in all.

GEORGE

That does it! Must be over a hundred cases. What do you think, Al?

AL

Easily 400, maybe 500. Good thing there was lotsa driftwood. The tarp was too small.

GEORGE

Look at these! '83 Cote-Rotie! '71 D'Yquem Sauternes! Beautiful! Whoever brought these in knows wine! Something's strange.

AL

What is?

GEORGE

The cases are mixed. There's usually one vintage per case.

AL

Must be the special packaging.

PEGGY

Lynn says they're valuable.

GEORGE

Many are over $100 retail. This '67 D'Yquem is easily over $200.

AL

Wow!

GEORGE

Shall we have some? Should be drunk now, according to wine guide.

PEGGY

What do you think these are worth? *(Lynn puts bottles on cupboard.)*

GEORGE

400-500 cases? Easily $400,000. Maybe half a million!

LYNN

Aren't you going to call someone? You should give them back.

GEORGE

(*Stunned*) Give them back?

Peggy, George and Al talk together interleaved/overlapped.

PEGGY

Are you kidding, Lynn?

AL

Put it out of your mind!

GEORGE

Be serious, Lynn!

LYNN

They don't belong to us.

PEGGY

Who would we give them to? Why should we give them up?

LYNN

Peggy, they….

AL

If we report these they'll think we're the ones that brought them in.

LYNN

No, they….

GEORGE

These were abandoned and lost. These are found goods.

LYNN

Yes but….

9

PEGGY

We found them! Finders, keepers! Losers, weepers!

AL

They're probably illegal. We could get in trouble for smuggling.

GEORGE

We saved them from destruction. They'd a been smashed or sunk.

LYNN

It's your (civic) duty to return them.

GEORGE

Duty? It's our duty to save these for mankind. They're priceless.

AL

Mankind?

GEORGE

Most I ever had in my cellar was 25 cases. This is 20 times as much.

LYNN

It's stealing! You could go to jail! Tell them, Peggy!

PEGGY

They wouldn't put us in jail. *(Hesitates.)* Would they?

AL

Let's just hide them 'til this blows over.

PEGGY

I agree. Besides, who'll know we have them?

LYNN

Won't the "owner" come looking for them?

AL

Those guys are coming here looking for the wine? We've had it!

LYNN

Shh, Al. Well?

PEGGY

They'll think the boat sank. For all they know, the whole cargo went down with the ship.

LYNN

They're designed to float. They must've planned to smuggle them in somewhere.

PEGGY

But didn't plan on a strong current?

AL

Wow! It's all a plan to bring them in here!

LYNN

This area used to be a great place for smugglers. Right?

PEGGY

Oooh! This is getting exciting. Smugglers!

AL

Smugglers' cove. Here! *(Pirate's chuckle ad lib.)*

PEGGY

The crooks are sure to come looking for their goods – their booty.

GEORGE

No one could possibly appreciate these as much as me – as we could!

LYNN

I know, George. I understand how much this means to you.

GEORGE

You'll never find most of these – ever. They're really rare.

LYNN

(Puts arm around him.) It's OK. We'll think of something, I promise.

AL

What'll we do?

LYNN

We need some creative thinking. (*Pacing.*)

PEGGY

Why don't you unpack the boxes? That way, they'll take up less room.

AL

That's a great idea! My big truck can take all that stuff to the dump.

GEORGE

Let's get to work! (*They start to leave, energized again.*)

LYNN

Where'll you put the wine? You can't leave it on the beach! What if they search for it?

AL

How'll they know where it went?

LYNN

They know what it is and that it floats.

PEGGY

It's only a matter of time before they figure the direction of the current.

AL

Yeah, when nothing shows up on shore....

GEORGE

Hmmm! I wonder. It's a lot of bottles to hide. (*Looks around.*)

AL

What about that room off to the side of the kitchen?

GEORGE

The laundry room? No that's too small. (*He moves toward bedrooms.*)

LYNN

Forget it, George! Not my bedroom! Not the house at all! Find some place outside.

GEORGE

OK. We've got until morning to figure this out. Let's get moving!

PEGGY

Look! See the light far down the beach. Someone's walking the shore.

AL

They're on to us. It's over. *(He peers from behind Peggy.)*

LYNN

Quiet, Al! *(She looks over their shoulders.)* What's he doing?

PEGGY

He's coming this way. He's looking at all the houses.

GEORGE

Is he still on the shore? *(Looks from behind Lynn. All four in a row.)*

PEGGY

Yes. No. He's walking slowly up here.

LYNN

George, turn on the beach floodlights. *(He does.)*

PEGGY

That stopped him. He's not moving. *(They stand motionless.)*

LYNN

(Pretends to talk on cell phone. Loud.) Hello? Sheriff? We have a prowler outside. Come quickly. A gun? Yes, we have a GUN. You'll be here in two minutes? Good. We'll wait. Get here quickly.

PEGGY

(Looking.) I think he heard you. He's leaving.

13

AL

He'll be back. I know it! We're in deep trouble.

GEORGE

Where's he going?

PEGGY

Back down to the beach.

LYNN

Good. That's a relief.

PEGGY

Wait! He stopped. He's turning. I think he has a gun.

AL

Oh no. He's not fooled. He'll find the wine.

PEGGY

He's coming back. Wait! He's going around toward the garage.

AL

We left the side door of the garage open. He'll get in. We're done for.

GEORGE

Shush, Al! I have an idea. Come with me.

George goes into kitchen, Al to kitchen doorway, Lynn to front door.

PEGGY

He's gone. (*Peggy runs to front door, stands behind Lynn, peers out.*)

GEORGE

(*Off. Shouts from "outside" door to garage.*) Is your shotgun loaded?

AL

Yes. (*George pulls Al in. Says "louder". Al yells.*) YES, LOADED!

GEORGE

(*Off.*) Let's go get him. (*They stomp feet, bang, rattle door.*)

LYNN

He's not there. He's coming to the front door. *(George runs in and stands behind Peggy.)*

GEORGE

(Al follows and stands behind George. All peer out. Loudly.) Are you ready to shoot?

AL

(Finally gets it. Loudly. Out door.) If he so much as twitches, I'll blow his head off.

LYNN

He's leaving.

PEGGY

Running up to the street. Oh, Al, well done. This is really exciting.

GEORGE

That was close. Let's get going. We don't have much time to move that wine.

George, Peggy and Al file out to the beach. Lynn stays behind.

LYNN

Heavens! What've we gotten ourselves in for? *(She slowly follows them. Fade.)*

Pantomime (SL to SR - optional): Lights dim, backlighting only. Midnight. Four figures in silhouette tiptoe along beach, opposite from before. Each carries an unopened box of wine, taking it from the stash.

15

Scene 2

Fast scene change. It's the next day, late morning. Lighting is much brighter than previous scene. Al enters from the garage via the kitchen. Lynn hears him and enters from the bedroom wing. They are very tired from being up much of the night and look it.

AL
Done! I was alone at the recycle area. Where're Peggy and George?

LYNN
Hiding the wine bottles. Better put these away. Help me Al.

AL
Why? What's wrong?

LYNN
They're hot. Someone might show up.

They put 10 of 12 bottles in cupboard. Knock at front door interrupts.

AL
Oh! The smugglers! They're here already.

LYNN
Keep quiet. I'll do the talking. (*He cowers behind her.*)

AL
We're finished!

LYNN
(*Lynn opens the door.*) Come in!

Mrs. Herald enters. She is a humorless busybody. As soon as she comes in, her eyes are everywhere. She takes in every detail, the consummate snoop.

MRS. HERALD
Did you see what happened?

AL

Who, us? *(Pokes out from behind her.)* Where?

MRS. HERALD

Last night on the water. You have a better view than I do.

Goes to telescope. Notices two bottles which they forgot to put away.

LYNN

Mrs. Herald? You just moved in a few houses down - across the street?

MRS. H.

Did you see anything?

AL

(Peeks out from behind Lynn) Nothing!

LYNN

My husband and I were reading. *(Mrs. H looks at Al.)*

AL

I'm her neighbor!

LYNN

We didn't look at the water. What happened?

MRS. H.

It looked like a boat was having trouble. *(She snoops around.)*

AL

What'd you see?

MRS. H.

Not much, I don't have any binoculars.

AL

A boat? Must be your imagination. After drinking a little…

MRS. H.

I don't drink! Strange you didn't see it. It was there some time.

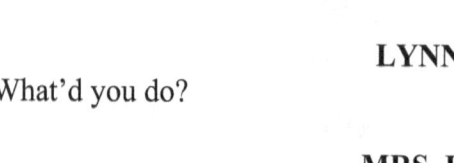

LYNN

What'd you do?

MRS. H.

Called 911. Passed to the Coast Guard. Sure you didn't see anything?

LYNN

No, of course not!

MRS. H.

They called me back. Never found the boat. Seems someone across the pass also called.

LYNN

Oh? What about?

MRS. H.

Reported two men swimming for shore. Coast Guard picked up one.

LYNN

One of them?

MRS. H.

The other one disappeared. They couldn't find him. *(Snooping.)*

AL

He's coming to get us! *(Sotto voce.)*

LYNN

Did they say anything else?

MRS. H.

No. Only the man was under investigation. *(She drifts to door.)*

LYNN

That's it?

MRS. H.

To tell them if I see the other one. Asked me to keep my eyes open.

LYNN

Keep your eyes open? Why?

MRS. H.

If anything floats ashore. Better get going. Sorry you missed it. *(Exits)*

AL

They must know everything! What are we going to do now?

Mrs. Herald pops back in quickly as if to hear something. She looks around as if she missed something. She notices the wine again.

MRS. H.

I forgot one thing. They mentioned wine. Terrible, evil stuff!

AL

Wine?

MRS. H.

If any on that boat, I hope it's destroyed. I should check the beach.

Dashes out to beach. Lynn chases after her and yells in vain.

LYNN

That's OK, there's nothing out there.

MRS. H.

(Pops back.) You were reading. How'd you know? *(Exits to beach.)*

AL

What if that guy squealed, about the wine?

LYNN

Stay calm, Al! I'll handle everything. *(Peggy and George enter.)* We had a visitor!

PEGGY

Who?

LYNN

Our new neighbor Mrs. Herald. What a snoop!

AL

She doesn't like wine.

LYNN

She's looking for something. George, you need to hide all these.

Lynn opens cupboard, grabs several bottles to give to George and Al.

AL

Why? You expecting someone?

LYNN

(She nods.) Help me Peggy.

George and Al are loaded with 5 bottles each.

PEGGY

Open your strong arms wide, fellas!

LYNN

Where'd you hide the wine?

GEORGE

In our woodshed behind all the wood. It's cool and dark there.

PEGGY

They'll never find it. It's a good hiding place.

LYNN

You better hide these too. *(She tries to give them the 2 visible bottles.)*

GEORGE

This is all we can carry. We need some to drink anyway. *(Al & George exit via kitchen.)*

LYNN

These can't sit out. *(She puts the 2 bottles in the cupboard.)*

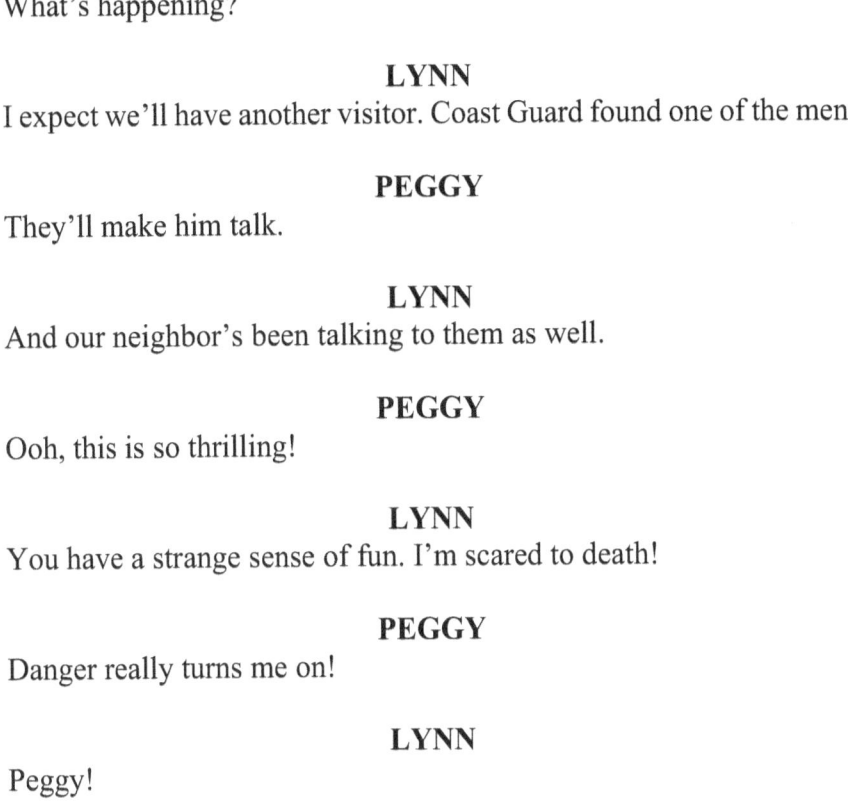

PEGGY

What's happening?

LYNN

I expect we'll have another visitor. Coast Guard found one of the men.

PEGGY

They'll make him talk.

LYNN

And our neighbor's been talking to them as well.

PEGGY

Ooh, this is so thrilling!

LYNN

You have a strange sense of fun. I'm scared to death!

PEGGY

Danger really turns me on!

LYNN

Peggy!

PEGGY

I remember one night last year. Al and I were walking along the road. We were fooling around and I got him all hot. I was draped over a mailbox with my clothes around my ankles. Suddenly a car raced around the corner with the headlights hitting us full beam.

LYNN

My Lord!

PEGGY

We were like two deer, frozen. They screeched to a stop.

LYNN

What'd you do?

PEGGY

I hopped into the woods, my clothes around my ankles. Al after me.

LYNN

I don't want to hear any more!

PEGGY

I can't remember being so turned on! Don't you and George do things like that?

LYNN

This is exciting enough for me. (*Al and George return via kitchen.*)

GEORGE

That's that! (*Looks around.*) What happened to the other two bottles?

Before Lynn can respond, the "Wine Owner" bursts in the front door.

WINE OWNER

Sorry about barging in, but I'm in a hurry.

GEORGE

Who are you?

LYNN

What do you want?

W.O.

Never mind about that. Have you seen anything floating on the water?

GEORGE

Now, see here! Who do you think you are, barging in here?

He moves toward the Wine Owner who steps back and pulls out a gun. Lynn stops George with a hand. The W.O. is holding the gun awkwardly showing he is unfamiliar with guns.

W.O.

Take it easy! Just answer my questions and no one'll get hurt.

PEGGY

What do you want?

W.O.

I'm looking for something. Have you seen anything?

LYNN

No, we haven't!

AL

Nothing!

GEORGE

What're you looking for?

W.O.

Never you mind!

AL

(*Blurts out.*) Our neighbor across the street saw something and called the Coast Guard! They could be here any minute!

WO hesitates, starts to front door, drops gun, picks it up, exits.

PEGGY

Al!

AL

I thought that might get rid of him. It worked!

PEGGY

What're we going to do now?

W.O.

(*Off.*) Bloody hell! (*Shots are fired. Voice yells stop.*)

WO runs in front door waving gun wildly, runs into the bedroom.

LYNN

What's he doing in the bedroom?

WO runs back into the room, looking a bit panicky and bewildered.

W.O.
Don't move! Which way to the beach?

AL
(*Al points toward the beach exit.*) That way!

W.O.
Don't say a word! Bloody hell! (*Runs across room, exits to the beach.*)

LYNN
Do you think he knows what he's doing?

AL
Who knows! I'm glad he left. He'll shoot someone the way he's waving that gun around!

PEGGY
Wow, Al, this is really getting so exciting! (*Arm around Al.*)

GEORGE
We hid the wine just in time! *(More shots.)*

AL
Who's doing all that shooting outside?

LYNN
Probably the sheriff. Everyone stay put. Act natural. *(They pose.)*

A Coast Guard officer comes in the open door. She looks around. Al points toward beach. She runs toward beach, runs in, out front door.

COAST GUARD LADY
(*Off*) Headed up the beach!

VOICE
(*Off*) We see him! (*She comes back in out of breath.*)

CGL

I'm Susan Wasserman. Coast Guard. Sorry for disturbance. You OK?

LYNN

We're fine! What happened?

CGL

We've been watching for him! Thought he'd head here. *(Notices Al.)*

AL

Who is he? Why are you after him? *(Peggy sees CGL staring at Al.)*

CGL

I'm glad he didn't harm anyone. *(Smiles at Al.)*

LYNN

Why's the Coast Guard involved?

AL

(Drifts behind Lynn.) What'd he do?

CGL

We're just helping. It's now a job for the sheriff. They'll catch him.

GEORGE

Woods are thick there. *(Points.)* Aren't you afraid he'll escape?

CGL

We have his truck – he can't go far! Besides, this is an island. *(Honk. She yells.)* Hold on a minute! I'll be right back. Don't go anywhere.

AL

Where would we go?

CGL

I need to ask you some questions. *(She leaves.)*

AL

(Al calls after.) We don't know anything.

MRS. H.
(*Off. Returning from beach.*) You hoo.

PEGGY
Hello, Mrs. Herald.

MRS. H.
I walked all along the beach. Couldn't find a thing.

AL
(*Sotto voce.*) Well, that's a relief!

MRS. H.
Someone ran past me on the beach. What's that about?

PEGGY
A jogger. That's big around here. I jog; they jog; don't you jog?

CGL
(*Off*) You go with the sheriff! I'll be along after I ask some questions.

AL
(*Behind Mrs. H. Points to her.*) They're going to ask lots of questions.

LYNN
Mrs. Herald, this'll be serious. It's better if they don't find you here.

MRS. H.
Oh, I don't mind. Maybe I can help.

LYNN
(*Edges her toward kitchen door.*) Hide her in the kitchen, George.

He pushes her into kitchen, shuts the door and stands in front of it.

GEORGE
Where're the other two bottles of wine?

LYNN
In the cupboard. (*She points.*)

26

CGL

(*Enters.*) Hello again. Seen anything unusual, especially on the water?

AL

Nothing! (*CGL smiles at him. Peggy blocks CGL view of Al.*)

GEORGE and LYNN

No, not a thing!

CGL

Anything floating?

LYNN

No, why? Should we be looking for something?

CGL

A boat sank last night and we think the cargo floated ashore.

AL

Our neighbor saw a boat on the water in trouble.

CGL

Do you mind if I look around? It's routine.

Doesn't wait for answer, starts searching house, exits to bedrooms.

PEGGY

Al, I love you but you talk too much. I'm sorry. *(Arm around him.)*

CGL returns. Looks around, but doesn't look in the cupboard where Lynn has put two bottles. She goes to kitchen door. George blocks it.

GEORGE

Just the kitchen. (*She pushes him aside and goes in.*)

The CGL returns, shuts the door and turns to them.

CGL

By the way, the Sheriff'll stop by to ask questions. *(Flirts with Al.)*

She exits back out the front door. The four of them look at each other.

PEGGY
What happened to Mrs. Herald?

LYNN
(Looks in kitchen.) There's no one in the kitchen. She's gone.

GEORGE
Probably went straight out through the garage. Close call.

AL
It's just a matter of time. The jig's up.

GEORGE
Shush, Al!

Al, George and Peggy talk together interleaving/overlapping.

PEGGY
What are we going to do?

AL
Give it back! They're on to us. Just a matter of time! We're doomed!

PEGGY
Don't be silly, Al! They probably don't know much. Besides, I'd rather throw it back into the water. What's next?

GEORGE
Too late to give it back. We have to find a good hiding place. It'd be a crime to throw it back! A lifetime's collection of fine wine! Think!

LYNN
I have an idea!

They stop talking. Before she tells her idea, shots ring out on the beach. The harried and disheveled Wine Owner enters, panting.

W.O.

Don't move! (*Waves gun, looks at kitchen door.*) What's in here?

GEORGE

It goes to the garage. Straight through! (*W.O. heads to kitchen door.*)

W.O.

If you tell them where I went, you're all dead. (*He exits to garage.*)

They don't know what to expect. There is a brief silence.

LYNN

He isn't very good at escaping. Must be an amateur crook.

GEORGE

Maybe we should help him escape.

AL

We can't get rid of him. He still has a gun. It's no use. Just confess.

GEORGE

Al, keep quiet.

PEGGY

All these smugglers, gun shots, danger! I can't stand any more of this!

LYNN

Peggy! Just calm down, all of you. Let them catch him if they can.

The CGL runs in from beach. Before she utters a word, Al points to front door. She runs out. Lynn goes into kitchen. Others don't move.

GEORGE

Quick thinking, Al!

AL

You think I want to get killed!

LYNN

(*Lynn returns quickly.*) He's gone!

GEORGE

He must've left out the back.

LYNN

George, what happened to the Chablis? It's not in the kitchen.

AL

It was when we came through. I remember.

GEORGE

Yeah, sitting right next to the opener.

LYNN

The opener's not there either. Sure you didn't put it in the wine cellar?

GEORGE

No. Where'd they go? (*Dashes into the kitchen.*)

PEGGY

Maybe that crook took it!

George backs slowly out of the kitchen followed by a staggering Mrs. Herald. She carries the bottle of Chablis Grand Cru now almost empty. She takes a swig from the open bottle.

GEORGE

(*He cries out.*) My Chablis!

MRS. H.

(*Slurring her words.*) It's not yours anymore. It's mine!

George tries to take it from her. She clutches it and pulls it away.

LYNN

Never mind about your Chablis, George! Get her home before someone else shows up.

MRS. H.

I can go home by myself. (*Tries to take a swig but can't manage it.*)

LYNN

Al, help George. Be discreet, George. Don't let anyone see her.

GEORGE

Shall we put a bag over her head? (*They exit with Mrs. Herald.*)

LYNN

She's getting to be quite a nuisance. *(Yells.)* Let her keep the bottle!

PEGGY

Before all this happened, you had an idea?

LYNN

Yes. They're determined to find something. We'll have to wait 'til dark. (*Goes to front door.*)

PEGGY

This is almost too exciting, even for me. (*She follows Lynn.*)

LYNN

This'll also keep Mrs. Herald out of our hair. Here's my idea. (*Exit. Fade.*)

Pantomime (SR to SL - optional): Lights dim, backlighting only. Three figures in silhouette tiptoe along the beach, opposite from last time. Each carries an open box with wine sticking up, taking it from the woodpile to Mrs. Herald's barn and Al's house.

Scene 3

It is late evening, same day. Fast scene change. Lights are low. Lynn is on her cell phone, handkerchief over mouth, deep voice and accent.

LYNN
This the Sheriff? I'm reporting suspicious activity. Yes! Three people carrying boxes from the beach. I'm sure! To a barn! I saw them in the dark. I don't want to get involved. *(Hangs up. Peggy enters via beach.)*

PEGGY
(She is covered with leaves and twigs.) I'm quite a mess, aren't I?

LYNN
My heavens! What happened to you? It's late. Where've you been?

PEGGY
Having an incredible time! I barely escaped! *(Removes leaves, twigs.)*

LYNN
After moving the wine to her barn, I went to the lookout corner. You weren't there but a car was. You look like you've been in the woods.

PEGGY
I'll say! *(She looks at the door.)* Is that car still there?

LYNN
No! It left some time ago. I looked for you but then I gave up.

PEGGY
Good idea. Never would've found me. What an adventure!

LYNN
Well, tell me what happened!

PEGGY
That car was coming so fast. I had to stop him.

LYNN
Why?

PEGGY

Before he saw the wine. I didn't know what to do. So I flashed him.

LYNN

You what!?

PEGGY

I flashed him. (*She opens her coat, mimes lifting a top or sweater.*)

LYNN

You must be insane!

PEGGY

Didn't you ever do that? We did that all the time in high school.

LYNN

You're crazy. What happened?

PEGGY

He screeched to a halt. Then he got out. Then my coat dropped.

LYNN

You mean you dropped it! Then what?

PEGGY

He took a step. My heart was pounding. I was tingling all over.

LYNN

Peggy! You're absolutely mad! I don't know what to believe with you.

PEGGY

You can believe this! Another guy got out. Both started after me. It got hotter than I could handle, so I ran like hell through the woods.

LYNN

Where'd you go?

PEGGY

Up the beach. I've been out there a long time working my way back.

LYNN

I wonder who they were?

PEGGY

I've no idea! They gave up and went back to the car, I guess.

LYNN

I don't know whether to think of you as a hero or a madman!

PEGGY

Try sexy heroine who almost gave her all for the cause. I have to admit it was exhilarating. If it was just one guy I may have let him catch me!

LYNN

Peggy!

PEGGY

Just kidding. How about something to warm me up?

LYNN

I opened one of those bottles a while ago. George likes it to breathe. *(Gets it from cupboard, goes to kitchen.)* It should be ready by now.

PEGGY

Wonderful!

Lynn returns, fills two glasses, puts the bottle back in the cupboard.

LYNN

You could use some wine. You look pretty ragged.

PEGGY

I am. This should help. *(Lynn gives her the glass.)* Where are the guys?

LYNN

Moving the rest of the wine to your cellar. Should be here any minute.

Al and George enter, disheveled and tired. George brings one more bottle from the stash. He gives it to Lynn. She puts it in the cupboard.

34

GEORGE

We finished moving the rest of it. We'll seal it up tomorrow.

AL

How many cases are in her barn? It took you a long time to sort it out.

GEORGE

About 50 cases. One of the hardest things I've ever done.

PEGGY

What's that?

GEORGE

Giving up all that wine! I tried to give up lesser vintages.

AL

Kept your favorites: Côte Rôtie, Latour, Rothschild *(Mispronounced)*.

GEORGE

Yes, but there were some beautiful wines in those other 50 cases.

AL

You still have at least 350 cases. Or maybe I should say - I do!

PEGGY

We do.

AL

Lynn, why do you think they won't look in our cellar?

LYNN

They'll be happy with the 50. They don't know how much there was.

PEGGY

I hope you're right. I could use a break from all this excitement.

LYNN

You? You said you loved danger. You said..

GEORGE

What did you tell them on the phone?

LYNN

Just enough for them to be suspicious and go to her barn. Let's have a toast! I'll get two glasses. *(She exits to kitchen for two more glasses.)*

AL

I hear cars on the road. That's funny! We don't usually have traffic this late at night! *(Looks out.)* Someone's coming! *(Runs in and sits.)*

Lynn brings two glasses from kitchen, puts them on cupboard, goes to front door. CGL comes to front door, doesn't come in since Lynn stands in way to discourage her from seeing the others too closely.

COAST GUARD LADY

We caught the man that was here earlier. *(Works her way in.)*

LYNN

Wonderful! We heard two men were reported last night. Is this one?

CGL

No, it couldn't be. We picked up one for questioning and have a description on the other. We'll find him soon. *(She sits near Al.)*

AL

Who's this one then? *(CGL stares at Al. Moves closer.)*

CGL

Local wine dealer, think he's part of a smuggling ring.

LYNN

A smuggling ring? Here? Amazing! Where'd you find him?

CGL

Caught him doubling back. On his way to your neighbor's house.

LYNN

Our neighbor? Across the road?

CGL

Yes. He gave the sheriff trouble. Put up quite a struggle.

PEGGY

Wow! A smuggler! Glad you caught him.

CGL

He yelled "If we don't let him go, Mr. Big will take care of us." Odd.

PEGGY

Mr. Big?

CGL

Yes, did he mention a Mr. Big when he ran through here?

AL

Oh no!

CGL

Did you know the sheriff received two phone calls?

AL

Two phone calls? From whom? *(CGL touches his knee.)*

CGL

First from a neighbor reporting a suspicious car with two men in it.

PEGGY

A car with two men? Here? *(Pushes in between CGL and Al.)*

CGL

At the corner with the motor running. Did you hear anything?

AL

Oh, no! Not a thing!

CGL

They had something to do with this. One maybe the man that got away. Sheriff's looking for them. He has a brief description of the car.

LYNN

You say there were two phone calls?

CGL

The second was strange. They had information. "Didn't want to get involved". *(Mimics)*

PEGGY

Do you know who called?

CGL

No. Had a cheap cell phone. Hung up. But we did follow up the tip.

GEORGE

What tip?

CGL

About your neighbor Mrs. Herald! The sheriff found a large quantity of wine in her barn.

AL

Wine? She didn't look like a wine lover!

CGL

Also a large quantity of wine in her. Drunk!

PEGGY

Amazing!

GEORGE

You said a large quantity of wine? In a barn? How much?

CGL

Don't know yet. Sheriff's confiscating it. Pick it up in the morning.

GEORGE

In the morning?

CGL

Then we'll do an inventory. Looks like quite a big stash.

LYNN

Why's he confiscating it? Is there something wrong?

CGL

It's evidence. Mrs. Herald's been arrested. We think she's the ringleader of a smuggling operation we've tried to uncover. *(Points outside.)* She's just been taken into custody.

MRS. HERALD

(Off. Yells) How dare you hold me! I demand my rights. I'm innocent. I'm being framed.

VOICE

(Off) You'll get a fair hearing. We'll go easy if you tell us who helped.

LYNN

You never know about people do you? Never would've suspected her.

MRS. HERALD

(Off) This is the way you treat someone when they help you!

VOICE

(Off) Where'd you get this wine? Just tell us the names of the gang…

MRS. HERALD

(Off) What wine? I don't know anything about any wine, or any gang! I'm going to get a good lawyer and sue you for false arrest, if you don't let me go! I'll sue the Coast Guard and the police and the sheriff. Who are you? I'll sue you too? *(Leaving. Fading.)*

CGL

I'd better join them. I'm sorry about this morning if I was too abrupt.

PEGGY

No problem.

LYNN

About this smuggling ring, do you know how big it was? How many people involved?

CGL

We haven't figured that out but we think there were four or five. We have three of them in custody. Don't worry. Won't be long before we have them all behind bars. *(CGL exits.)*

Lynn gets glasses, wine from the cupboard. Others talk together.

AL

Can you believe it?

PEGGY

Incredible! Mrs. Herald!

GEORGE

I wish I could hear the rest of that conversation!

PEGGY

(Mimics Mrs. H) I demand my rights. I'm being framed! I'm innocent!

AL

(Gruff – deep – voice .) That's what they all say!

GEORGE

(Mimics) I don't know anything about any wine or gang! I'll sue you and everyone else!

AL

The mob's lawyers are gonna be pretty busy. *(Three of them laugh.)*

LYNN

Why's the Coast Guard giving us this inside information? I hope they're not on to us.

PEGGY

Stop worrying so much. She's a little too friendly to Al. But I'll put a stop to that.

GEORGE

Cops bought it so far. They think they have ringleader, most of mob.

PEGGY

Looking for two men. Think they'll have the whole ring pretty soon!

AL

(Giggles) Sheriff found large quantity of wine in her barn, lots in her.

LYNN

What if there really is a Mr. Big?

PEGGY

Oh, Lynn, you're not serious! He just made that up.

LYNN

I'm dead serious. Coast Guard, Sheriff think they have the ringleader.

GEORGE

Well, so what?

LYNN

What happens when they find out Mrs. Herald is innocent? I bet those two in the car were Mr. Big and the missing guy. They're stalking us.

AL

They're on to us. Mr. Big is gonna wipe us out.

GEORGE

Al, shush! Let's think about this. If there is a Mr. Big, what does he want? He doesn't know yet how much wine the sheriff confiscated.

AL

Yeah, but he knows how much there was, and when he finds out...

PEGGY

How does he know how much there is. For all he knows it all sank.

GEORGE

Peggy's right. Let's not worry too much.

Lynn pours two glasses of wine for George and Al, refills other two.

41

LYNN

I guess you're right. *(To George.)* It's been open 45 minutes! OK?

GEORGE

Perfect! How did you know?

LYNN

You'd think I'd learn a few things being around you. Let's have that toast! *(They raise their glasses)* To the end of the smuggling ring!

AL

To good neighbors! And my wine collection! *(Peeks at George.)*

PEGGY

To a thrilling adventure! We should do this more often!

GEORGE

To Latour, Pomerol, Côte-Rôtie, Chambertin…!

They raise their glasses together, clinking glass to glass. Peggy raises her glass to drink and there is an extra clink. They stop at this unexpected sound. Peggy looks in her glass to see what made the sound. She reaches in and pulls out a small shiny glittering object.

PEGGY

What's this? I could have choked on this. *(Holds up "stone" in light.)*

GEORGE

Terrible! Ruining a fine wine by sloppy bottling. How could they?

AL

(Takes a drink.) Not bad! Mine's OK. No rock's in mine!

LYNN

That's not a rock, you fool! A blue one! Very rare! *(Gets her 10 power loupe from the cupboard. Peers into it.)* Superb clarity! Flawless! The cut is magnificent, well-proportioned! *(Holds it.)* Just under 15 carats, I'd say. Extremely valuable! You know what this is, Al?

AL

It's not a rock? *(Stares at it.)* Looks like one!

LYNN

I've never seen one as beautiful as this! *(Holds it up.)* Oh, my heavens!

PEGGY

What is it, Lynn? What's wrong?

LYNN

It's exquisite. Missing diamond cut from the 110 carat Tavernier Blue.

GEORGE

What's that? *(Stares at the diamond in Lynn's hand.)*

LYNN

Given to Louis XIV. Cut down to 69 carats. Renamed the Blue Diamond of The Crown.

GEORGE

Louis XIV? That's old.

LYNN

From that came the Hope Diamond and a 14 carat blue. This is it.

AL

(They gather round, stare.) Those old stones? Are they worth a lot?

LYNN

The Hope weighs 44 carats, worth $200 million. What do you think?

PEGGY

Oh, no! This is what Mr. Big really wants! It's not the wine he's after!

AL

You know, I heard a clink like that when we were moving the wine.

PEGGY

(Shrill.) When, Al, when? When did you hear the clink?

43

AL

Last night I think. I really didn't think much about the clink.

GEORGE

(Frantic.) Where, Al, where? Where did you hear the clink?

AL

I don't know. Could've been anywhere.

PEGGY

Think, Al, think! We've gotta find the clink.

AL

(Hesitates.) I think it must've been the barn.

LYNN

It doesn't matter.

PEGGY

What do you mean? It's not too late. The wine's still in the barn.

LYNN

We have to search everything. Who knows how many there are?

AL

Mr. Big knows!

GEORGE

Let's get started. We have 'til morning before they take the wine away.

AL

Let's finish this wine first. It's not too bad.

Al finishes his wine, then Peggy's. Lynn finishes hers. George pushes his away. Al finishes George's glass while Lynn refills Al's and Peggy's glasses. Al promptly drinks them. George, resigned and saddened, moves to the door to go check the wine in the barn.

LYNN

George? *(Holds up empty bottle.)* You might look for more of these.

44

GEORGE

This is too much! A lush drinks my beautiful Chablis Grand Cru then some idiot ruins my fine Côte-Rôtie with some old rocks. Disgusting!

LYNN

This isn't an old "rock" George. I may not know wine like you but I know my stones. This is worth far more than all that wine put together.

GEORGE

(He *comes closer and stares at it.*) How much?

LYNN

Millions! If we find more, we'll have a fortune. *(She puts the empty bottle in the cupboard.)* You can lose a few bottles of old wine. Besides, the wine's still good, isn't it?

PEGGY

We'll help you, George. We only have a few hours. Come on Al. Let's get started. *(They hook arms gently with his and start out.)*

AL

Yeah, before Mr. Big gets here. *(To Lynn)* You coming?

LYNN

I'll be right along. I want to look up some things.

AL

Wait. What shall we look for?

LYNN

Tilt each bottle gently and listen for a small clink. *(She demonstrates.)*

As they start out, the house phone rings. No one moves. They all suspect who's calling.

AL

(The phone rings insistently.) He's coming! We're doomed! What are we gonna do?

GEORGE and PEGGY

Shush, Al!

The phone keeps ringing but no one will answer it. Fade out.

End of Act One.

Pantomime (SL to SR then SR to SL - optional): Lights dim, backlighting only. Three figures in silhouette tiptoe along the beach opposite from last time. They are not carrying anything. Then two figures in silhouette tiptoe back along the beach, returning.

Alternate pantomime (off to side - optional): Lights dim, backlighting only. Three figures tilt and shake wine bottles looking for diamonds. They find three in pantomime. Then two figures in silhouette tiptoe along the beach to the other site and one leaves.

ACT TWO

It's early the next morning. As the lights come up dimly, Lynn is seen going through magazines, in particular The Journal of Gemmology, and Gems and Gemology. She is wearing a housecoat over PJs. The magazines are scattered. She tosses George's wine magazines around the floor, far and wide, with relish, to get to the bottom of the rack to find her gem magazines. As she peers into one, she stops, listens, and looks around. She remembers the bottles in the cupboard, goes to it, pulls out three bottles, one of which is empty, looks around, tries to decide what to do with them, and finally goes to the kitchen.

While she is out, Peggy enters through the front door, wearing her bathrobe. She is clutching three diamonds in her hand, each wrapped carefully in tissue paper. She holds them as if they were eggs. Peggy looks exhausted. Lynn comes back in without the bottles. Lynn also looks tired. Both have been up two straight nights and are showing it. Peggy looks around at the small mess of scattered magazines.

PEGGY
What've you been doing?

LYNN
I hid the wine bottles in the laundry room, in case someone pops in.

PEGGY
Good idea. No. I mean all this. (*Points at magazines strewn around.*)

LYNN
Trying to find articles in gem magazines about missing diamonds.

PEGGY
Missing diamonds in these wine magazines you scattered all over?

LYNN
(*Ignores the crack.*) You look terrible.

PEGGY
You would too, if you'd been up all night.

47

LYNN

I have been. Remember? *(Looks her over.)* Why're you wearing that?

PEGGY

My lookout outfit. I was on duty. Good thing. We almost got caught.

LYNN

What happened?

PEGGY

We finished with the bottles when I saw a flashlight coming our way.

LYNN

What'd you do?

PEGGY

Ran back inside, doused our lights, ducked in back and hid.

LYNN

And then?

PEGGY

Someone was trying to get in. A car drove up and they ran away.

LYNN

Lucky. Where're Al and George?

PEGGY

At our house going through the rest of the wine.

LYNN

Did you find anything?

PEGGY

(With glee.) Sure did! Three gorgeous diamonds! *(Holds them out.)*

LYNN

I knew it! There must be more. (*Takes them, looks at them through the loupe. Holds one up.*) Oh, no! This is not a coincidence!

PEGGY

What is it? What's wrong?

LYNN

Incredible! (*Takes the other blue one from a pocket and looks at the two together.*) The identical dark blue color. Between 6 and 7 carats.

PEGGY

What's that mean?

LYNN

The Brunswick Blue. Cut from the French Blue along with the Hope.

PEGGY

Another famous missing diamond, I take it?

LYNN

Yes. The blue's extremely rare. Priceless! (*Holds four in her hands.*) Someone knows their diamonds! Were they all in the '83 Côte Rôtie?

PEGGY

Only two of them. One was in an '86 Latour. George was furious.

LYNN

What I thought. Must be lots of diamonds. I wish I knew how many.

PEGGY

I thought that's what you were doing.

LYNN

There're many missing diamonds. I just need to figure out which are being smuggled.

PEGGY

What diamonds are missing?

LYNN

Many of the French Crown jewels, stolen in 1792, were never recovered, including eight of the Mazarins. The famous Florentine diamond was stolen in Austria in 1920.

PEGGY

Wow! And they never found them? (*She moves toward the computer.*)

LYNN

And Iranian Crown jewels. The infamous Darya-i Nur, stolen in 1984.

PEGGY

(*Sits down.*) How can you tell one diamond from another?

LYNN

Clarity, weight, cut and color. The Florentine was a shade of yellow, the Darya-i Nur a shade of red. Each diamond has a unique internal identity. What're you doing?

PEGGY

Did you see that article posted on the web a few days ago?

LYNN

No, what about it?

PEGGY

About shadowy figure operating in Europe and Middle East. Poses as wine dealer. He's trying to acquire missing diamonds, legally or not.

LYNN

How do they know about him?

PEGGY

Interpol, but he dropped off their radar screen. Stays one step ahead

LYNN

Who is he? What's his name? Does it say?

PEGGY

Here it is. He's part French, part Pakistani. Goes by Pierre Abdul.

LYNN

He just disappeared?

PEGGY

(Reads) Known to be accomplished pilot. Authorities think he flew across a border to escape detection. Knows he's being watched.

LYNN

Maybe he has a mole in Interpol or somewhere tipping him off.

PEGGY

An insider? You have a great imagination, Lynn. A mole!

LYNN

Maybe he's Mr. Big. Not missing at all. Maybe he's right around here.

PEGGY

Looking for his diamonds? *(Knock at door. She peeks.)* It's her again. *(Lynn looks for hiding place. Sticks four diamonds in bowl of agates.)*

LYNN

I need a better place to hide these.

PEGGY

You talk about me living dangerously.

LYNN

Come in! *(The Coast Guard Lady enters.)*

CGL

I came by to warn you. *(Seems to be looking for something. Al?)*

LYNN

What about?

CGL

A lawyer posted bail for that wine smuggler. We had to let him go.

PEGGY

Why warn us?

CGL

Might come here. Claims there's more wine. Isn't convinced it sank.

PEGGY

Heavens! I hope he doesn't think we know anything about it.

CGL

Do you?

PEGGY

Of course not.

CGL

If he tries anything, let us know. *(Looks around again.)*

LYNN

Sure thing!

CGL

Where's that cute shy guy?

PEGGY

That "cute" guy? Off somewhere looking "cute". And shy. Off-limits!

CGL

Tell him I said hello. *(Starts to leave.)* Oh, one other matter.

LYNN

What's that?

CGL

Released your neighbor. Prosecutor didn't feel we had a strong case.

LYNN

Well, you did the best you could.

CGL

We tried. Oh, have you heard any unusual activity out there?

PEGGY

No, why?

CGL

Last night our patrol saw someone trying to get into the barn.

LYNN

Maybe it was the wine smuggler.

CGL

It couldn't be! He was in custody. *(Keeps looking around.)*

PEGGY

Man or woman?

CGL

Hard to tell. Could've been either.

PEGGY

What'd they look like?

CGL

Strange you should ask. Big. Heavy set. Remember Edward G. Robinson in Key Largo?

PEGGY

Vaguely.

CGL

Like that but bigger.

LYNN

We'll be on the lookout.

CGL

I've got to be going. Help take the wine into custody.

PEGGY

Come again! *(The Coast Guard Lady looks Peggy over.)*

CGL

What's with the bathrobe? You having a sleepover?

PEGGY

(*Poses.*) I'm a model.

CGL exits thru front door.

LYNN

Peggy!

PEGGY

Just trying to be friendly.

LYNN

I don't like her coming here, poking around.

PEGGY

Why? What's wrong?

LYNN

Her behavior. It's not professional. It doesn't make sense.

PEGGY

What do you mean?

LYNN

Why's she telling us all this. Flirting with Al. She's up to something.

PEGGY

As long as she's not up to something with Al.

MRS. H.

(*Mrs. Herald enters from beach.*) Hello there.

LYNN

Why, Mrs. Herald, what on earth are you doing out there?

MRS. H.

Heard that smuggler guy's in jail. He's sure there's more wine.

PEGGY

I'm glad they let you out.

MRS. H.

I was framed. They didn't have a thing on me.

LYNN

Of course they didn't.

MRS. H.

Who put that wine in my barn? Have any idea who's out to get me?

PEGGY

Can't imagine why anyone'd want to do that to a nice person like you.

MRS. H.

That smuggler said there was lots of wine. What happened to it?
(*She looks around, takes an involuntary step toward the bedrooms.*)

LYNN

Maybe it sank in the deep water, or he's lying, trying to stir up trouble.

MRS. H.

I don't think so. He said it was all tied together. It couldn't have sunk.

PEGGY

It's a big mystery then. (*Noises coming from the beach. Barking dog.*)

W. O.

(*Off in distance.*) Bloody hell.

LYNN

Someone's coming! Could be dangerous. You'll be safe in kitchen.

MRS. H.

Why? What's so dangerous? (*The noises get closer.*)

PEGGY

Lots of guns and shooting lately. Hide in there. (*Motions to kitchen.*)

MRS. H.

Not again! You have any more of that white wine? That was good!

PEGGY

Come on! (*Hustles Mrs. H into kitchen, who exits before W. O. enters.*)

LYNN

What are you doing here?

W. O.

Out on bail. I want to ask some questions. *(Hands up.)* Look! No gun!

PEGGY

Well, I should hope not! Scaring people that way.

W. O.

Look, I don't want to scare anyone, I just want some information.

LYNN

We told you already, we haven't seen anything.

W. O.

The cops found some wine in a barn, so some of it got to shore.

PEGGY

Amazing!

W. O.

Someone put it there. Wasn't that lush. There's more than that.

PEGGY

If there was, maybe it all sank.

W. O.

I don't think so.

LYNN

We told the Coast Guard all we know.

W. O.

If I don't find that wine I'll have chains and concrete round my feet.

PEGGY

You mean?

W. O.

Yeah, that's right, at the bottom of that deep water out there.

LYNN

That's terrible! Who'd do such a thing?

W. O.

The boss, Mr. Big! He's mad as hell! I'm gonna take the brunt of it.

PEGGY

Who's Mr. Big?

W. O.

The big boss. Boys from Marseilles call him Le Blaireau!

LYNN

Le Blaireau?

W. O.

The Badger!

LYNN

The Badger? Not Mr. Big?

W. O.

I call him Mr. Big outta respect. The boys call him Le Blaireau, the Badger. That's how he looks – big, wide, heavy, strong, tough as nails.

PEGGY

What's he so mad about?

W. O.

He's looking for some special wine – certain vintages.

LYNN

Certain vintages? Like what?

W. O.

'83 Côte Rôtie, '86 Latour, and, oh yeah, '86 Mouton Rothschild. You wouldn't 'ave seen any of those, would ya?

PEGGY

Heavens no! We haven't seen any wine at all.

LYNN

Why those?

W. O.

Those are some of his favorite wines.

PEGGY

Well, I hope he finds them, for your sake.

W. O.

If I don't find 'em soon, I'm splitting. He don't mess around. He'll bump off anyone he thinks double-crossed him.

LYNN

If they dredge the water, maybe they'll find the wine.

W. O.

If some of that wine made it, it all did. It's somewhere around here.

PEGGY

(*Sound of someone approaching in distance. Dog bark*.) What's that?

W. O.

It's them damn cops again! Don't say nuttin'! (*Exits through kitchen.*)

LYNN

We better do what he says. Let them do all the talking.

PEGGY

Do you think he means what he says? About this Mr. Big?

LYNN

Probably. We can't take any chances. There's something strange.

PEGGY

What's that?

LYNN

I don't think he knows about the diamonds.

PEGGY

Only Mr. Big knows? How can that be if this guy's the smuggler?

LYNN

He's just a pawn in this. He thinks he's just smuggling wine.

PEGGY

You're right. *(Noises.)* Here comes my favorite person. *(CGL enters.)*

CGL

Thought I'd stop by to see how you're doing. Anyone been here?

PEGGY

(Quickly) No one!

CGL

Good! By the way, we caught one man. Trying to sneak into the barn.

LYNN

Great! Was it the same one they saw earlier?

CGL

No, this's the one that got away two days ago. We finally got him.

PEGGY

How do you know it was him?

CGL

The description! Thin and wiry. The other one was heavy set.

LYNN

Like a badger?

CGL

Yeah, come to think of it. How'd ya know? (*Keeps looking around.*)

LYNN

No reason. Just a guess.

CGL

If that wine dealer comes by, let us know. He's to stay clear of here.

PEGGY

Oh, we didn't know that. We will.

CGL

After we find one more we'll wrap it up. Keep your eyes open. *(Exits.)*

LYNN

Mr. Big was at the barn. He's still at large! Could be here any moment.

PEGGY

Oooh! This is sooo exciting!

LYNN

Peggy, not now! *(Thinks)* He's looking for the diamonds. The wine smuggler mentioned three vintages. From three cases? Think that means we need to find thirty-six diamonds?

PEGGY

Makes sense! Can I use your computer again?

LYNN

Yes. Why?

PEGGY

I've gotta check other articles on the web. *(Sits with computer.)*

Lynn picks out the diamonds from the agates in the large bowl of unpolished agates. She looks around trying to figure out where to hide them and hears noises of people coming. She hides them in the sugar bowl. Al and George drag themselves in the front door.

AL

We think we found all of them! (*He holds a pouch in his hand.*)

LYNN

(*Sotto voce.*) Shush Al. How many did you find?

GEORGE

(*Sotto voce.*) We counted thirty. What's the matter?

LYNN

Ears might be listening. Give me those! (*Al hands pouch to Lynn.*)

AL

You gonna look at them? (*Lynn adds four in sugar bowl to pouch.*)

LYNN

No time! We've got big trouble! (*Exits to the kitchen with the pouch.*)

GEORGE

What's going on?

AL

How should I know?

GEORGE

(*Yells into kitchen.*) What're you doing?

LYNN

(*Off*) Hiding everything in the flour tin – the big one that says Tea.

AL

Why? (*Lynn returns from kitchen.*)

LYNN

We've had lotsa visitors, and we're gonna have one more!

PEGGY

Found it! Just what I thought. Googled old wine, diamonds and smuggling.

GEORGE

It's not old wine, it's aged.

LYNN

What did you find?

PEGGY

Interpol says "large number of diamonds smuggled out of Europe, flawless, D color, a few rare fancy coloreds, some famous missing ones, extremely valuable. Be on the lookout!"

LYNN

Incredible! We've got really big trouble!

GEORGE

Hold on a minute! Just what's been going on here?

LYNN

(Very fast dialogue.) The Coast Guard came by.

AL

Not again!

PEGGY

That smuggler's out on bail.

AL

Mrs. Herald?

PEGGY

No the real smuggler.

LYNN

They also let Mrs. Herald out.

PEGGY

That was Mr. Big at the barn.

GEORGE

How do you know?

                    LYNN

From the description.

                    AL

We're doomed!

                    LYNN

Mrs. Herald was here snooping.

                    PEGGY

She's looking for wine.

                    LYNN

The smuggler came by looking for wine.

                    PEGGY

He doesn't believe us.

                    AL

We're really doomed!

                    GEORGE

Al, shush!

                    PEGGY

The Coast Guard came back.

                    LYNN

They caught someone.

                    PEGGY

But not Mr. Big.

                    LYNN

He's looking for diamonds.

                    GEORGE

What on earth's going on?

PEGGY

(Rapid.) Coast Guard came by and let the smuggler out not Mrs. Herald but the real smuggler and also let Mrs. Herald out and the smuggler came by looking for wine not Mrs. Herald but the real smuggler and Mrs. Herald came by looking for wine and Mr. Big was at the barn but not here and Coast Guard came by and caught someone at the barn not Mr. Big and he's looking for diamonds not wine.

GEORGE

How much are all these diamonds worth?

PEGGY

They said $100 to $200 million, even $250 million. They're not sure.

GEORGE

A quarter of a $billion? It would take an awful lot of wine to beat that.

AL

It's all over. We're finished!

LYNN

Oh, shush Al! Did the article say how many diamonds there were?

PEGGY

It says there are thirty-six diamonds.

LYNN

I was afraid of this. We're missing two. Go back through them again.

PEGGY

What do you mean?

LYNN

We have 34 out of the 36. There're two missing.

PEGGY

Where are the 34 diamonds?

LYNN

I hid them in the flour but we need a better place.

Mrs. Herald staggers out of the kitchen holding a bottle of red wine.

MRS. H
Wasn't any more white wine but this red's pretty good. *(Slurring.)*

LYNN
Oh no, not again!

MRS. H
What do you expect if you keep hiding me in there.

PEGGY
We put you in the kitchen.

MRS. H
That's no place to hide! That side room's cozy. *(Noises outside front.)*

LYNN
(Lynn takes the wine.) Al, hide this somewhere! *(He takes the wine.)*

AL
Sure thing! *(Starts to beach, changes his mind and goes into garage.)*

LYNN
And George, take her home! *(George and Mrs. H start out front door,)*

Wine smuggler enters with sawed-off shotgun or nunchucks.

W. O.
Hold it! Just hold it there! *(Mrs. H. puts her hands up.)*

MRS. H
Don't hurt me!

W. O.
I won't hurt anyone. Just relax. I want to get to the bottom of this.

AL
(Returns, hears last words.) Bottom of what? Oh!

W. O.

(*To Al*) Get in here. (*Throws ropes to Peggy.*) Start tying them up.

MRS. H.

Now see here! You can't do this!

W. O.

(*Produces a gag.*) And gag her too!

GEORGE

Now look here, you can't just barge in here waving nunchucks!

W. O.

Gag him too!

Peggy starts gagging and tying up Mrs. Herald and George first.

PEGGY

What are you going to do with me after I tie them all up?

W. O.

I'll get to you. Just tie them up and set them on the couch.

PEGGY

Ooooh, this is sooo, sooo exciting!

LYNN

Peggy!

PEGGY

Going to hold us hostage? For ransom? Not going to kill us, are you?

W. O.

I'm not killing anyone. No hostage stuff either. I just want to find that wine before the Badger gets here. If I don't get answers by then, I'll be wiped out along with all of you.

AL

The Badger?

LYNN

That's Mr. Big.

During this, W. O. directs Peggy to tie the others. George and Mrs. H. are gagged, sitting on couch with hands tied behind their backs. Al and Lynn sit next to them while Peggy is tying their hands also.

W. O.

(*The coffee table is pushed away from the couch. To Al*) OK, now talk!

AL

(*Blurts.*) Don't know a thing. Sheriff's looking for you and Mr. Big!

PEGGY

Why do they call him Mr. Big? Is it because…what I think? Oooh!

LYNN

Peggy!!

W. O.

A wise apple, aren't you? Mr. Big'll have something special for you.

PEGGY

What do you mean something special?

W. O.

(*Was kidding thinks quickly.*) Oh, I don't know. The feather treatment!

PEGGY

(*Takes the bait.*) The feather treatment?

W. O.

Yeah! Tie you down and tickle you with feathers until you talk.

PEGGY

Oh no! Not feathers! I couldn't stand that. Oh mercy! (*Bolts to beach.*)

W. O.

(*To others.*) Don't move! (*Chases her.*) Come back! Stop or I'll shoot!

The W. O. grabs her robe as she wriggles from it as she exits.

AL
(Whining.) We're doomed! We're all doomed!

LYNN
Oh, Al, be quiet and stop whining!

W. O.
(Returns, mumbling, throws the robe down in disgust. Bloody hell! *(Mrs. Herald is mumbling. The W. O. removes her gag.)*

MRS. H
I couldn't breathe. How dare you hold me like this? I demand my rights. First I'm framed and then locked up for no reason and now I'm tied up and gagged. Untie me at once, or I'll sue you. I'm going to get the sheriff and the Coast Guard and the police and my lawyer and...

He puts the gag back on, helps her to her feet, and leads her on her unsteady feet to the bedroom area. She resists but he insists.

W. O.
You're a pain. I can't deal with all this. *(Takes her to bedroom area.)*

LYNN
(Quietly.) Al, I hope Peggy's all right out there. Maybe she'll get help.

AL
Maybe. If she stays out of sight. She's pretty smart.

LYNN
Let's hope she doesn't run into Mr. Big.

AL
You OK, George? *(George shakes his head no. Tries to spit out gag.)*

W. O.
(Returns.) I wouldn't want to be married to that lush!

Checks that their hands are tied, puts a rope around them and couch, hangs up Peggy's robe. George mumbles. W. O. removes his gag.

GEORGE

Now see here. This is my house. You can't just barge in and do this. Untie us and leave this house immediately or you'll be locked up for years: breaking and entering, assault and battery, false imprisonment. I'll get my lawyer and sue you for every penny you…

W. O. puts the gag back on. Suddenly Mr. Big appears, as if from thin air. He is as described: big, wide, heavy, fierce, like a big badger. He moves quickly, with purpose. He seldom wastes time or words.

MR. BIG

(Brusquely) Did you find the rest of the wine yet?

W. O.

Le Blaireau! Mr. Big!

MR. BIG

I asked you a question.

W. O.

No, not yet, but….

MR. BIG

(Interrupts.) You mean to say you haven't found any wine yet?

W. O.

No, but it's under control. I'm just about to make them talk.

MR. BIG

You haven't even started the interrogation?

W. O.

No, but…

MR. BIG

(Gestures) These the ones that got my wine?

W. O.

Most of 'em. One got away.

MR. BIG

You let one get away? (*Menacing*)

W. O.

She was scared so she ran off. But I got her robe.

MR. BIG

Her robe? Why didn't you chase her and get her back?

W. O.

I couldn't leave them. They weren't tied up yet.

MR. BIG

What if she talks? Have you thought of that?

W. O.

She left her robe. She's not going far.

MR. BIG

Let me get this straight. You haven't found any wine, or questioned them, one got away but you couldn't stop her because they weren't even tied up yet. Tell me, what have you done?

W. O.

I got her robe. (*Holds it up.*)

MR. BIG

Her robe? Let me go through this again. No wine! No interrogation! You lost one. There's a woman running around (naked) because she's scared. All you have is her robe? What's she scared of? Not you!

AL

(*Rapid dialogue. Bleats out.*) Of you!

MR. BIG

Who?

70

LYNN
You.

MR. BIG
Why?

AL
He said you'd tie her up.

LYNN
Down.

AL
What?

LYNN
Down. Tie her down.

AL
And give her the feather treatment.

MR. BIG
The what?

AL
The feather treatment!

MR. BIG
The feather what? What the hell are you talking about?

W. O.
I was just kidding.

MR. BIG
You're useless! My boys will take you for a ride. I'll make these punks talk if I have to drop hot coals down their shorts. Why's he gagged.

W. O.
He was jabbering.

71

MR. BIG

Take it off! (*He does.*)

GEORGE

I demand you release us. Leave my house before it's too late. I'm going to get the sheriff and the Coast Guard and the police and my lawyer and…(*Mr. Big puts the gag back on.*)

MR. BIG

What's he been drinking? My wine?

LYNN

(*Quickly.*) No, his own.

MR. BIG

Let me see the bottle! Where is it? (*Al eyes garage. Lynn kicks him.*)

VOICE

(*Off*) OK, surround the house.

W. O.

Jeez, the cops! What are we gonna do, boss?

MR. BIG

I'll tell you what you're gonna do! Take the nunchucks, walk outside with your hands up. You're gonna take the fall! Go on. Move!

W. O.

(*Reluctant to go.*) Ya gonna bail me out again, boss?

MR. BIG

You're lucky I don't shoot you myself! Outside! (*WO exits slowly.*)

AL

It's no use. You're surrounded! You might as well give up.

MR. BIG

That's what you think! Where's that go? (*Points to kitchen.*) Quick or I'll shoot!

LYNN

To the garage. (*He runs out.*)

VOICE

(*Off*) Drop that gun. Hands up. I said drop that gun or we'll shoot.

W. O.

(*Off*) Don't shoot!

VOICE

(*Off*) Watch out! Duck! Get the gun! There he goes! (*Shot fired.*)

W. O. runs in front door, out to beach. More shots fired. He runs back in and front of couch where Al trips him with his foot. He sprawls across floor, rolls out front door as Al jumps up and down with glee.

CGL

(*Off*) Someone's rolling out the door. He's got a gun. Watch out.

VOICE

(*Off*) That's him again. Grab him.

CGL

(*Off*) Get that gun. Cuff him. (*Quiet.*)

AL

I guess they got him.

LYNN

Nice job, Al! How'd you get him to roll out the door? (*Al shrugs.*)

VOICE

(*Off*) Take him away. You're doing time for this, fella.

CGL

(*Off.*) Put him in the car. I'll be right back. (*Comes in. Runs to Al.*)

LYNN

Thank heavens you came! None too soon.

CGL

(*Throws arms around Al. Softly.*) Are you OK?

LYNN

We're all fine. (*Struggles in bonds. The CGL notices.*)

CGL

Was he the only one here? (*Unties Lynn.*)

AL

Another guy was. He split.

LYNN

(*Points.*) In the garage. Be careful! (*CGL leaves. Lynn unties others.*)

CGL

(*Returns.*) He's gone! (*Ungags George.*) When did he leave?

AL

A few minutes ago. Didn't you see him? (*She runs out.*)

CGL

(*Off. Yells.*) He went that way. (*Enters.*) We're going after him. (*Exits*)

LYNN

Poor Mrs. Herald. Where is she? (*Lynn exits to bedroom area.*)

GEORGE

At least she won't find any wine in there!

AL

He was kinda rough on Mrs. Herald, don't you think? We've been too.

GEORGE

Rough on her? What about me? Wonder what's happened to Peggy?

AL

Oh, she'll take care of herself. She runs like a deer.

Lynn enters with Mrs. H. who is still groggy.

LYNN

She was tied to the toilet. Take the gag off Al. *(He does.)* Take Mrs. Herald home George. And no bottle!

GEORGE

(Takes her.) Help me, Al! *(Starts out slowly.)*

MRS. H.

(Slurred.) My bottle. It's not empty.

LYNN

Wait! Let her keep it. Where is it, Al? *(Al exits garage.)*

GEORGE

What for? My good wine! *(Al returns with bottle of red half full.)*

LYNN

Never mind! Just do it. I have my reasons. *(They exit.)*

Lynn sits down, very tired. Peggy comes slowly in from the beach. She is wearing one of Al's hunting shirts. It comes down to her knees.

PEGGY

Well, I guess it's safe now.

LYNN

I see you found something to wear after you left your robe.

PEGGY

I grabbed one of Al's hunting shirts.

LYNN

Where've you been?

PEGGY

I crept to Al's truck and used his cell phone to call the sheriff.

LYNN

The cops got here just in time but Mr. Big got away.

PEGGY

Mr. Big showed up? Oh, no!

LYNN

You're lucky you escaped. He was mad. If he catches you, watch out!

PEGGY

Oh Lynn I can't stand the feather treatment. What are we going to do?

LYNN

We need to throw them off, confuse them and keep Mrs. Herald busy.

PEGGY

Everyone's suspicious. What did you have in mind? Maybe I can help.

LYNN

George'll have to give up more wine. He won't like it but we've got to move it tonight!

PEGGY

Oh, Lynn! Not again! We're all exhausted.

LYNN

We've got to do it! There's no choice. *(Fade.)*

End of Act Two.

Pantomime (SL to SR - optional): Lights dim, backlighting only. Two figures in silhouette tiptoe along the beach, opposite from P3. Each carries an open box with wine sticking up, taking it from Al's house to Mrs. Herald's house.

ACT THREE

It's early the next morning. Lights are dim. Lynn wears a bathrobe over her peignoir. She's on her cell phone, handkerchief over her mouth and a different accent than before.

LYNN

Is this the sheriff? I'd like to report a burglary. Yes! That area near the Pass. What? I saw two people going in and out of a house. Yes, I'm sure! A barn? No, not a barn. A house near a barn! Yes, I was walking in the dark early when I saw them. No, I don't want to. I'm afraid.

Lynn hangs up. Peggy enters via beach wearing short shirt and new shoes. She's covered with leaves and twigs. Removes them slowly.

LYNN

That should do it.

PEGGY

That's getting to be a habit, isn't it?

LYNN

You should talk! Where have you been?

PEGGY

Here and there.

LYNN

New running shoes?

PEGGY

My new improved lookout outfit. Know what happens if I bend over?

Peggy starts to bend over to show Lynn. Lynn holds up her hand.

LYNN

That's enough. I think I can imagine.

PEGGY

Well, when we started stashing the wine at Mrs. Herald's, I tested it.

LYNN

You tested it. How?

PEGGY

I bent over in front of Al. George saw me and dropped two bottles.

LYNN

Oh, Lord! Peggy!

PEGGY

Al just smiled but I knew it would work if I needed to use it.

LYNN

Well? Did you need to?

PEGGY

The guys were stashing the wine. I was on lookout and heard a car.

LYNN

Well? What happened?

PEGGY

Just as the car came round the bend, I touched my toes (*demonstrates*).

LYNN

Peggy! What happened?

PEGGY

The brakes screeched, and they ran into a tree.

LYNN

They?

PEGGY

Yeah, bad luck! Two guys climbed out. Two strong, fast deputies!

LYNN

Oh, Peggy! Someday you're going to get caught.

PEGGY

I hope so. Just kidding. Boy, were they angry, yelling, chasing me.

LYNN

How'd you escape this time?

PEGGY

Same as before. They came after me. I swear I outran a couple of deer.

LYNN

Apparently, you got away without being caught.

PEGGY

It was dark. They kept tripping over branches. I heard them cursing.

LYNN

What about the guys, Al and George? Where are they?

PEGGY

Must've heard the noise and lay low. Should be done. Better get them.

They start toward the front door just as Al and George stagger in from the garage. They're exhausted. They've been up three nights in a row.

LYNN

You guys look terrible!

George is in the worst shape. Lynn helps him to the sofa, Peggy helps Al to the sofa. George notices Lynn's short peignoir. Al sees short shirt Peggy wears to the top of her thighs. Both are revived.

AL

George almost didn't make it. He was so wiped out he dropped a couple of bottles.

GEORGE

Hardest thing I've ever done, giving up that beautiful wine. A crime!

LYNN

You still have at least those 350 cases. That should be enough.

GEORGE

Deciding what to keep of all that beautiful wine. That was really hard.

AL

He's really depressed. And he's really worn out.

LYNN

Did you find the other two diamonds?

AL

Nope. Not a one. Shook every bottle. No clinks!

LYNN

Did you finish? Did you move everything?

AL

Yep. All done! Every single bottle. Except the cases in our cellar.

PEGGY

They won't miss those?

AL

They'll never notice, especially with those broken bottles all over.

PEGGY

More broken bottles?

LYNN

I asked them to make a trail of broken glass.

AL

George couldn't bring himself to make the trail. I had to do it.

LYNN

From the barn to the house?

AL

Yeah, right up to her back door. It's not that great a distance. I didn't need many bottles.

PEGGY

I didn't hear any noise.

LYNN

How would you know? You were running through the woods again.

AL

Don't worry. There's no house nearby. Besides I was very quiet.

LYNN

What about the old lady?

AL

Zonked! Never moved an inch when we put that wine under her bed.

LYNN

And in the closets?

AL

And in every cupboard.

PEGGY

And in the bathrooms?

GEORGE

And the laundry room, and garage, and bedrooms.

AL

Another job by Al and George. We should go into business. Wine movers! Anytime!

LYNN

George needs some sleep. Al, do you mind taking him to your place?

AL

Why my place?

LYNN

He'll never get any sleep here. I'm sure we'll have many more visitors.

PEGGY

Never mind, Al! I'll take him. I need to change clothes anyway.

LYNN

You mean you need to put…

PEGGY

Come on, George, I'll give you a hand. *(Peggy helps him stumble out.)*

GEORGE

I've been up for days.

AL

Only three nights. Get back soon. We may need to move more. *(Exit.)*

LYNN

Al, I'll need your help but why don't you rest now. *(Exits to bedroom.)*

Al falls asleep instantly. CGL enters, looks for possible hiding places. Sees Al asleep, looks at him adoringly, hears Lynn's voice on the bedroom phone, starts to pick up house phone and hears Lynn say "goodbye". The CGL moves to the door and shuts it as if entering.

CGL

Anyone home? *(Al jumps.)*

AL

Oh, hi! Didn't hear you.

CGL

Thought I'd see how you're doing. You had quite a scare last night.

AL

Oh, it was nothing!

Lynn enters. CGL continues mild flirting with Al through this.

LYNN

I didn't hear you come in.

CGL

Had a call about two guys near the barn. Sent a couple of deputies.

LYNN

Did they find anything?

CGL

They saw a trail of broken glass, found wine bottles stashed all over.

AL

Wine? What did they do?

CGL

Stacked 'em up. Sheriff'll do inventory in morning. His jurisdiction.

LYNN

In the morning? Did they find anyone?

CGL

Found occupant Mrs. Herald drunk. We're now convinced of her role.

LYNN

Her role?

CGL

The ringleader. But there's more including a female accomplice.

AL

Did they arrest her?

CGL

She ran into the woods. This's a big mob. So, we've devised a plan.

AL

A plan?

LYNN

You have a plan?

CGL

We're adding more deputies. Then we're gonna let out a decoy.

AL

A decoy?

CGL

More like a pigeon. We're letting out that wine smuggler on a pretext.

LYNN

A pigeon?

CGL

Actually two pigeons. After we sober her up, we'll let out Mrs. Herald.

AL

If they're guilty, why are you letting them out?

CGL

To lead us to the mob. (*To Al.*) Thanks for being so helpful, so brave.

AL

Brave? No problem here!

CGL

We'll be nearby. We're watching the old lady's house. (*Exits.*)

AL

That's a relief to know!

LYNN

I think we're the decoys! More like "bait". I don't like it. Not one bit.

AL

(*Al sits on sofa, dazed.*) I'm pretty tired. I don't think I can help much.

LYNN

That's OK, Al, take a nap. I'll work on this myself.

Lynn goes to kitchen to examine the diamonds. Fast scene change.

Lights dim then come up brighter showing passage of time. Al is fast asleep. His shirt's undone. Lynn returns with pouch in one hand and diamond in the other. She's removed her robe and still wears her short peignoir. She stares at diamond in rapture and adoration, holds it up to light. Hears a noise, puts pouch and diamond in sugar bowl. The sheriff enters via front door. Lynn puts her finger to her lips - "shh".

SHERIFF
(*Sotto voce.*) Hello. I'm Sheriff Connery. (*Lynn takes him far from Al.*)

LYNN
(Sotto voce.) Yes. I know. I'm the one that called you.

SHERIFF
You're right to be suspicious. We've had our own for some time too.

LYNN
I'm glad. I thought I was imagining it.

SHERIFF
No you're not, but we haven't any proof yet. You need to be careful.

LYNN
I will.

SHERIFF
I'll be nearby.

Exits through front door. Lynn gets diamonds out, looks at the last one and puts it in the pouch. She makes a loud noise, eg. moving chair.)

LYNN
That does it! The last one! *(Al awakens with a jolt.)*

AL
Last one of what?

LYNN
I've identified most of them. Found many known to be missing.

85

AL

Missing?

LYNN

We have one of the eight Mazarins, the Great Harry, the nine from the Great Cross of Francis I and six V Cut Roses from Louis XVI's Ceremonial Sword. They're priceless.

AL

How priceless?

LYNN

Doesn't matter. They're stolen. Can be easily identified, never sold.

AL

What's the point of finding them if we can't sell them?

LYNN

Al, these are international treasures and should be found for mankind.

AL

Mankind? You're starting to sound like George.

LYNN

Besides their historical importance, they're beautiful.

AL

Then all you can do with these is look at them.

LYNN

Al, you're hopeless. (*She puts the pouch in the cupboard.*)

AL

I guess wine's better after all. At least you can drink it.

Peggy bounces in from beach wearing Al's sweatshirt over shorts.

PEGGY

Boy, that shower was great! I feel like a million bucks!

                    AL
My sweatshirt!

                    PEGGY
I just borrowed it for a little bit.

                    LYNN
Is George sleeping?

                    PEGGY
Zonked. Out cold. Still asleep when I left. What's going on?

Al looks at Lynn. Very fast dialogue.

                    AL
We're decoys.

                    LYNN
The Coast Guard was here.

                    AL
We're waiting for Mr. Big.

                    LYNN
To step into the trap.

                    PEGGY
What trap?

                    AL
The wine dealer's out.

                    LYNN
He'll lead the cops to the mob.

                    AL
Mr. Big's just part of it.

                    PEGGY
What mob?

87

LYNN

They let Mrs. Herald out as a decoy.

AL

She's the ringleader.

PEGGY

They found all the wine?

AL

And Mrs. Herald.

LYNN

Al and George are part of the mob.

PEGGY

Part of what mob?

AL

You're an accomplice.

PEGGY

Then they suspect us?

LYNN

No, no, there's no mob.

PEGGY

No mob?

LYNN

They've mistaken you three for the mob.

AL

There's really only Mr. Big and the wine smuggler.

LYNN

So we're the decoys.

PEGGY

I'm confused.

AL

(*Rapid.*) The Coast Guard came by and Mr. Big is still on the loose and they want to set a trap for him and we're the decoys so they let the smuggler out not Mrs. Herald but the real smuggler so he'll lead them to the mob and they think George and I are part of the mob and you're an accomplice and Mrs. Herald is the ringleader so they let Mrs. Herald out as a decoy and they found all the wine but we're not the mob there's only Mr. Big and the smuggler so we're the pigeons.

PEGGY

My Lord!

GEORGE

(*George enters from the beach.*) Wow! I'm a new man!

LYNN

What a difference! Peggy said you had a nap.

GEORGE

It wasn't a long one but it helped. It was great! Except for the dream.

PEGGY

What dream?

GEORGE

I was tied up and gagged and surrounded by wine but I couldn't drink any of it and there were people running all over and gunshots and a big guy and I kept moving wine…

LYNN

It wasn't a dream, George. Anyway, glad you're feeling better.

AL

I never had any dream like that.

LYNN

(*Gets pouch from cupboard.*) Got to find a good hiding place for this.

89

Mrs. Herald enters via front door. Lynn puts her hands behind her back. Motions to Peggy to take the pouch. Peggy does and sits down.

MRS. H
Hello. Sorry to barge in.

LYNN
Mrs. Herald! It's a surprise to see you here. How are you feeling?

MRS. H
I'm fine now. I wanted to thank you two guys for taking me home.

GEORGE
Oh, do you remember?

MRS. H
I remember everything!

AL
Everything?

MRS. H
Everything, that is, until I passed out.

LYNN
I hope you're feeling much better now.

MRS. H
I'm not. I woke up in jail. I don't like it there. *(Tears.)* It was awful.

LYNN
(Moves toward her.) I'm sorry. Were they tough on you?

MRS. H
They said they found a lot of wine in my house, and in me.

PEGGY
A lot of wine in your house? Amazing!

MRS. H

They brought me in for observation they said. I know better.

LYNN

What do you mean? Why would they do that?

MRS. H

They're looking for the rest of the mob. They think I'm the ringleader.

PEGGY

Terrible!

MRS. H

I yelled, what mob, what wine, what ringleader?

LYNN

What an ordeal! You poor thing!

MRS. H

They must've believed me 'cause they let me go. I came straight here.

GEORGE

Why'd you come here?

MRS. H

(Starts to cry.) To see if you know who tried to frame me.

PEGGY

(Puts an arm around her.) We're so sorry someone would do that.

LYNN

How awful! Whoever did that was really mean!

AL

You shouldn't have come. We're decoys. They expect those guys.

Noises from beach. Lynn hustles her to kitchen.

LYNN

This will be dangerous. We don't want you to get hurt. Quick! In here!

Lynn pushes her as she moves slowly. Footsteps are getting closer.

MRS. H
This again! Getting to be a regular habit. (*She exits. Smuggler enters.*)

W. O.
Hands up! (*He waves his gun. All raise their hands, except Peggy.*) You, too! Stand up! (*She reluctantly stands.*) Hands up, I said!

She lifts her hands with the pouch in one of them, trying to hide it by putting her hands behind her head. He sees it. She flips it to Al.

AL
You better not stay here. They're looking for you. *(Flips it to George.)*

W. O.
(*To George.*) What's that? Let me see. (*George flips it to Lynn.*)

GEORGE
Oh, nothing!

W. O.
(*To Lynn*) Give it here. (*She tosses it to Peggy. He tries to grab it.*)

LYNN
It's Peggy's.

W. O.
I'll take that.

PEGGY
Just my imitation pearls.

W. O.
I'll decide what it is. Give it here! (*He grabs it. Mr. Big enters.*)

MR. BIG.
Never mind looking. I'll take that. (*He reaches for the pouch.*)

PEGGY

My pearls!

MR. BIG.

I think I know what they are, and they're not your pearls!

He grabs the pouch. He motions them with his gun to positions closer in, where he can keep an eye on them. George is next to Mr. Big at one end of the couch, Al is next to Wine Owner at other end, Lynn is behind the couch and Peggy is in front of it to one side of the coffee table. Peggy pretends to see something in the bowl of agates.

PEGGY

Oh, what's that? You must have left one of the diamonds here.

Peggy moves slowly to keep all eyes on her. She reaches in to the agates, pulls out a shiny one that has some glitter and fire, puts it in the palm of her other hand but lets it fall on the floor in front of the coffee table. With her back to Mr. Big, she bends over to look at it. Her sweatshirt rides up above her (short pants). She holds the pose for a moment. The Wine Owner and Mr. Big have followed her moves, and slowly turn to gape. Their jaws drop and they lower their guns. George and Al look at each other and get the same idea.

GEORGE

Now, Al, now!

George knocks gun from Mr. Big, wrestles with him while Al knocks gun from Wine Owner. Mr. Big escapes out the front door but in the struggle with George loses the pouch. It drops on the floor. Lynn slides it under the sofa and yells.

LYNN

George, he's getting away.

George follows him while Al grabs the Wine Owner around the waist.

PEGGY

Take him down, take him down.

Peggy jumps on his back. Lynn also throws herself on top of him while Al holds his ankles. He swings around with Peggy's and Lynn's legs and arms flying. He's brought down on Al who slides out from under before he's pinned. Peggy sits on the W. O. so he can't get up. Lynn picks up both guns and starts out after George.

VOICES
(*Shouts from outside.*) There he goes! Wait, there's another one. Don't shoot. Hold your fire. He got him! Good job! Move in!

AL
They got him!

Lynn turns back in, points a gun at W.O. while Al helps Peggy get up. W.O. rises slowly. George staggers in filthy and disheveled.

GEORGE
He was tough.

PEGGY
What happened?

GEORGE
I got him!

AL
(Mimics W. O.) They don't call him the Badger for nothing!

LYNN
George, you dear! (*Helps him sit. To W.O.*) Outside, you! *(They exit.)*

PEGGY
(Sidles up to Al.) Oh, Al! You were awesome! You took him down!

AL
You weren't too bad yourself. What a trick you pulled! *(Lynn returns.)*

LYNN
George, you were so brave! So fearless! Taking on Mr. Big like that! He's fierce!

GEORGE

Someone had to stop him. Al and I got the idea at the same time.

LYNN

I mean chasing him and tackling him. I'm so proud of you!

PEGGY

And you saved the diamonds!

LYNN

(Ruefully.) Yeah, for posterity, for everyone to enjoy, not for us alone.

PEGGY

At least you held them in your hands. (*Looks around.*) Where are they?

LYNN

(Motions under couch.) Leave them. They're better there for now.

PEGGY

Something wrong? (*Lynn shakes her head yes. The CGL enters.*)

CGL

Good job, all of you! Thanks for everything you've done.

AL

No problem.

CGL

In case you didn't know, there's a reward for catching the Badger.

AL

The Badger?

CGL

Interpol knew he was smuggling diamonds. The wine dealer was an unwitting pawn.

LYNN

Diamonds? Incredible!

CGL

Somehow the wine dealer discovered the real smuggling was the diamonds in the wine.

PEGGY

In the wine? Amazing!

AL

Ingenious! What an idea!

CGL

Then he decided to double-cross the mob, but the Badger found out.

GEORGE

Double-cross? He could have been exterminated.

CGL

Anyway, we got everything. Except the diamonds. I'll take them now.

LYNN

You mentioned a reward?

CGL

Unfortunately, there's no reward for recovery of the diamonds.

PEGGY

Why not?

CGL

These international treasures go back to Europe. You understand.

AL, GEORGE AND PEGGY

Oh!

CGL

But there's a reward for the recovery of the wine.

GEORGE

For the wine?

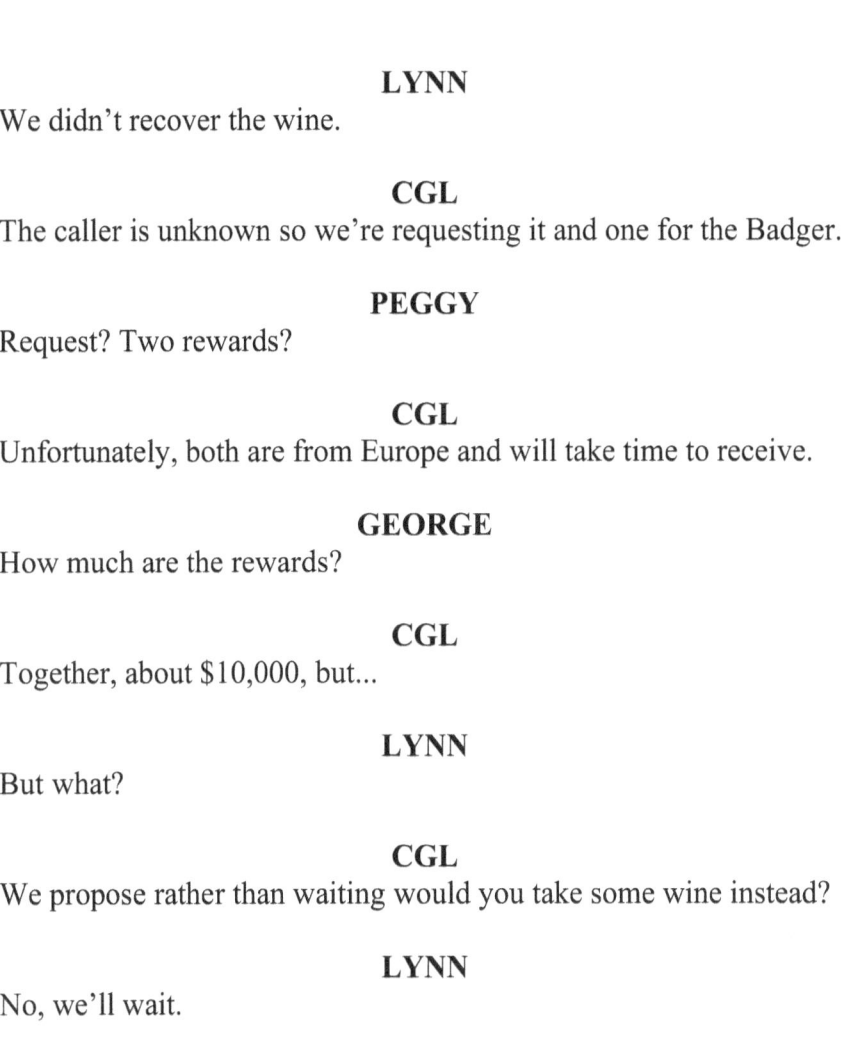

LYNN

We didn't recover the wine.

CGL

The caller is unknown so we're requesting it and one for the Badger.

PEGGY

Request? Two rewards?

CGL

Unfortunately, both are from Europe and will take time to receive.

GEORGE

How much are the rewards?

CGL

Together, about $10,000, but...

LYNN

But what?

CGL

We propose rather than waiting would you take some wine instead?

LYNN

No, we'll wait.

GEORGE

We'll take the wine.

CGL

How about 25 cases? That's the least we can do for all your efforts.

GEORGE

Can we pick out the wine?

CGL

I don't see why not. Go over to the barn now before they take it away.

GEORGE

I'll go down right away. Al, will you help me? *(They start out.)*

LYNN

Hold on. You can't do that. That's the sheriff's jurisdiction, you said.

CGL

I'm sure they won't miss a few cases. It'll be faster if you all go.

PEGGY

I don't know. Doesn't sound legal to me. Let's think about this.

CGL

Suit yourself. Where are those diamonds? I'd best be off.

LYNN

I don't know. We'll find them, get them to the sheriff soon's we do.

GEORGE

Oh, I know. Rolled under the couch during the chaos. *(He retrieves pouch, CGL reaches for it but Lynn snatches it.)*

LYNN

Great, George. I'll get them to the sheriff first thing in the morning.

CGL

It's OK. I'll take them into custody, get them to the proper authorities.

LYNN

I wouldn't think of it. I'll make sure they all get to the sheriff.

CGL

I'm afraid I'll have to insist. Turn them over. *(Reaches for pouch.)*

PEGGY

(Steps in front of Lynn.) Lynn's right. You're not the sheriff.

CGL

You're obstructing justice.

PEGGY
We recovered them. It's our responsibility to get them to proper hands.

CGL
(*Pulls out her gun.*) Hand them over now or I'll shoot.

LYNN
That's stealing. They don't belong to you.

CGL
They do now. I've waited a long time for this. Give them to me.

AL
She's right. Let's do what she says. Right, George? *(George nods. Al tosses pouch high, CGL looks up, Al flips pouch to Lynn, Peggy tackles CGL, George grabs gun, points it at CGL. Lynn calls sheriff.)*

CGL
(To Al.) I really like you. I'm not kidding, You're so nice.

AL
Tell it to the judge. *(To George.)* Let's take her outside.

CGL
(To Al) Don't you understand? I did this for you. Let me go, will you?

AL
If you so much as twitch I'll blow your head off. *(They exit.)*

LYNN
(*Calling.*) Sheriff? We have mole in custody. You are? Here? Good.

PEGGY
(*Peggy enters. Lynn hangs up.*) Sheriff drove up. Good timing.

LYNN
I know. I called him.

PEGGY
You suspected her?

LYNN

For some time. (*Lynn holds up pouch.*) We'll have to hand this over.

PEGGY

Too bad. You deserve something for saving them. (*Sheriff enters.*)

LYNN

You'll be wanting these beautiful gems. (*Lynn gives him pouch.*)

SHERIFF

Thanks. I wish I could give you a reward for these but I can't.

LYNN

We're happy to recover them. Our reward is just doing our civic duty.

SHERIFF

I've got to go and attend to the alleged perpetrator. (*He leaves.*)

PEGGY

(*Mimics.*) "Reward is doing our civic duty." Who are you kidding?

AL

(*Al enters.*) You gave him the diamonds. I saw the pouch. (*Lynn nods.*)

GEORGE

(*Enters.*) Did you tell him about the 25 cases? (*Lynn shakes no.*)

PEGGY

No, that's our reward.

LYNN

I guess we'll just have to settle for George's wine.

MRS. H

(*Enters via kitchen with glass, bottle red wine.*) This wine's no good!

LYNN

Why, Mrs. Herald, I'm sorry, we forgot all about you.

GEORGE

We also forgot about the other bottle! (*To Mrs. H.*) Why is it no good?

MRS. H

I poured my first glass. This time I took a long time. It's really good.

GEORGE

Then what's wrong with that wine?

MRS. H

Just as I was about to pour my second glass, I heard a clink.

ALL

A clink?

MRS. H

Yes, I think a piece of glass fell into the wine. It's ruined!

LYNN

Oh, don't worry! I think I can fix that problem.

She takes wine bottle from Mrs. H., and goes into the kitchen.

PEGGY

I'll help you. (*Peggy takes the empty glass, and follows Lynn.*)

MRS. H

I thought I heard noises out here.

GEORGE

Oh, nothing much! We caught the last crook. The sheriff has 'em.

MRS. H

Thank goodness!

AL

You're no longer a suspect. You can go home now.

MRS. H

Well, it's about time! Treating decent folk that way!

Lynn, Peggy enter with wine, five glasses. Lynn pours one for George.

PEGGY
(*Peggy pours one for Mrs. H.*) Try this one. I think you'll like it.

Lynn pours one for Al. Lynn then steps in front of George and bends over the coffee table to pass a glass of wine to Al. Her short peignoir rides high and produces the desired effect. George gulps.

LYNN
(*Peggy pours two more.*) To catching the thieves. (*Raise glasses.*)

PEGGY
To our good neighbor, Mrs. Herald. (*They drink. George sips.*)

MRS. H
Thank you. (*She gulps hers.*) I'd best be getting home.

AL
Maybe they missed some of the wine. Look around!

MRS. H
You think so? (*She brightens up at the prospect and starts to leave.*)

AL
Try the medicine cabinet. That's a good place.

LYNN
George, walk her home, will you?

MRS. H
No need. I can manage quite well, thank you! *(She exits.)*

AL
Did you find a diamond?

PEGGY
No, we heard a strange clink, but no diamond or glass in the bottle.

GEORGE

Hmmm. Let me take a look at that bottle. (*He goes into kitchen.*)

LYNN

What on earth's he doing?

PEGGY

I was going to propose a toast.

Holds her glass ready. Offstage crash. George returns.

GEORGE

Just as I thought. It was too big for the neck.

George shows shiny object. Rectangular, bit more than 1½ X 1 inch.

PEGGY

Where'd you find it then?

GEORGE

In the punt.

AL

The what?

GEORGE

In hollowed out false bottom called punt. Most bottles have them.

LYNN

(*Holds up pale pink diamond.*) George, you darling! You found it!

PEGGY

What is it? It's big! (*Lynn examines it and weighs it in her hand.*)

LYNN

Pale pink, flawless, rectangular step-cut, 180-190 carats. Darya-i Nur.

PEGGY

What makes you think so?

LYNN

(*Looks closely.*) Right color, right size. It was 41 mm by 29 mm.

PEGGY

I thought the Iranians claim they recovered the Darya-i Nur.

LYNN

Did they? Then no one will miss it, will they?

PEGGY

This calls for a special toast. *(Holds up her glass.)*

LYNN

To start of my diamond collection. As a necklace George?

Steps in front of George, pulls top down, puts diamond low in center.

GEORGE

Beautiful!

PEGGY

A toast! *(Holds glass.)* To sharing danger, secrets and friendship.

AL

To our wonderful wine collection. Guess it'll go in George's cellar.

GEORGE

375 cases! Most I ever had were 25. To sharing the wine. (*Drink.*)

LYNN

To the good things of life. *(Holds up diamond again.)*

GEORGE

Do you suppose this means I can't get that other wine now?

LYNN

Sorry! Come with me and you'll forget the wine. (*Lynn takes his arm.*)

PEGGY

You, too, Al, you brave warrior! Let's go home!

Peggy and Al move to front door; Lynn and George to bedroom wing.

LYNN
I wonder about that other diamond. Could it be..?

GEORGE
375 cases. That's 4500 bottles. A bottle a day. Should last 12 years.

LYNN
What if it's the Florentine? That's also too big. Light grayish yellow, flawless, fancy sancy cut, 137.27 carats, or the 60 carat Nur-ul-Ain.

Lynn exits after George.

AL
Maybe I should give you the feather treatment when we get home.

PEGGY
Oooh! Would you? If it's you, Al, I might do it.

LYNN
(*Enters.*) Al! George! Go to the barn. Go through all the bottles, shake them, look at false bottoms for a large diamond. Go now before they find it. Sheriff'll be here in the morning. (*George pulls her back in.*)

PEGGY
Would you blindfold me too?

AL
Sure thing.

George comes back out the open door. He smiles and shuts the door.

AL
I'll do what Mr. Big does. I've got some nice feathers. Tie you down.

PEGGY
Oh, Al! I can't wait. Will you be my Mr. Big? *(Drags him to door.)*

LYNN

(*Off.*) George! George, what are you doing? Oooh, Geoorge!

Peggy and Al smile. Lights dim very slowly as they move out door.

LYNN

(*Off.*) Geooorge, oooooh! (*Fading.*) Geoooooorge!

Silence. _End of Act Three._

Encore Pantomime (optional): Lights dim, backlighting only. Mrs. Herald is seen miming the opening of medicine cabinet, finding wine and opening it, drinking some, hearing clink, removing false bottom and taking out the Florentine "diamond". She looks at it and tosses the "rock" away and resumes drinking from the bottle. Lights out.

End of Play. Curtain call.

Appendix A – Prop List

Telescope
VHF radio
Phone on desk (land line)
Lap top computer
Cell phone
Tea service (sugar bowl)
Magazine rack with wine magazines and gem magazines
2004 Pocket Wine Guide
Bowl of agates on coffee table
Bottle of Chablis
2 bottles of red wine (different labels)
Big tan tarp
Sealed boxes (wine) – entre-act pantomimes
10 bottles of wine (different labels)
1st gun for W.O.
Open boxes of wine – entre-act pantomimes
Open bottle of wine (in cupboard; to be poured)
6 wine glasses (in kitchen or cupboard)
1st gem (in glass)
10 power loupe
1 consumed bottle of wine in cupboard (no intermission)
3 gems wrapped in Kleenex (different colors and shapes)
(Optional) Binoculars and walking stick for Mrs. H
Pouch with 30 gems
Half a bottle of red wine
2nd gun for W.O., ropes and gags
Gun for Mr. B
3rd gun for W.O.
Gun for CGL
Glass for Mrs. H and partially consumed bottle of wine
Glasses and wine
Last diamond

Appendix B - Author's Notes

"THE CONNOISSEURS" takes place on an island. It could be in the Pacific Northwest where smuggling has always been a way of life for some and a problem for others, as it is today. But many think this takes place on another island in another state. Could it be so?

Staging: Lighting is standard but dimming effects are essential. Scene changes must be as fast as possible, allowing minor set changes and lighting changes to show the passage of time. 5-10 seconds or less should be the goal. Each Act should have a continuous fast flow. As time goes on and characters have been up all night, they should show it. One doesn't look the same if one's been up all night or longer.

This play is fun to stage, to act in and to see. Intimacy with the audience is encouraged and is very effective, hence the suggestion in the script that the audience is positioned in the direction of the beach. Thus, in the case of thrust or proscenium, exits and entrances involving the beach can be through the audience, or via wings or curtain.

A walk through is essential to track flow and entrances/exits (on paper or with model of set, as well as a staged walk through). This should also include an overall schematic of the entire "crime" scene.

Quick changes: Quick changes must be rehearsed carefully. 10 seconds or less is the goal. Costume changes must be minimal.

Casting: A minimum of six actors is required (minimum two men). Sheriff can be off-stage. Double casting is possible for the minor characters. Since age and gender are not fixed for any of them, it is challenging and fun for actors and audience alike to have double casting. Several options are available to director. If casting of Mr. Big is different than description, the author authorizes minor changes to fit the actor.

Pacing, Rhythm and Intensity: The pacing in general should be quite fast, with some noted as very fast. There is a rhythm used throughout the play as in the up and down of waves coming to shore. There are slow quiet recovery moments, followed by heightened intensity and energy, and an even faster pace. High energy and a fast pace are essential.

The play is written with ample opportunities for physical and comedic action. The author encourages the director and actors to explore, develop and choreograph these.

Overlapped dialogue: These should be choreographed so that the dialogue appears to be simultaneous, but interleaved at a very fast pace so that all the dialogue can be heard.

By all means have fun while performing this play and the audience will also!!

www.ingramcontent.com/pod-product-compliance
Lightning Source LLC
Chambersburg PA
CBHW030550130626
46552CB00006B/2499